Bass Reeves
The Indomitable Marshal
Volume 1

Charles Ray

Uhuru Press

North Potomac, MD

For information about this and other works by this author, contact the author at charlesray.author@gmail.com

Cover art and design by the author.

Printed in the United States of America

ISBN-13 9798719522852:

Dedication

To the brave men and women of the U.S. Marshals Service, who have been serving the country since 1789. Created by the first Continental Congress, they are the oldest law enforcement agency in the United States.

Bass and the Preacher

The Marshal and the Madam

Renegade Roundup

INTRODUCTION

I first learned of Bass Reeves when I was doing research for my series on the Buffalo Soldiers of the Ninth U.S. Cavalry, and was fascinated with what I read. This legendary, but largely forgotten at the time, lawman was born a slave in Arkansas, ran away from slavery from Texas during the Civil War, and lived in Indian Territory (now Oklahoma) until war's end. As a slave, he'd been forbidden to learn to read or write, but during his stay in the territory, living among the Cherokee, Creek, and other tribes who had been forcibly relocated their under the Indian Removal Act, he became proficient in six of the tribal languages. In addition, he was an expert marksman, a dead shot with rifle or handgun shooting right- or lefthanded. He was an expert tracker, and after the war, when he'd returned to Arkansas, started a family, and operated a ranch, he was often hired by the deputy U.S. marshals out of the Western District of Arkansas and Indian Territory to scout for them when they went into the territory. Reeves was a big man, six-one or two and weighing over 200 pounds, much larger than the average man of the time, and with his huge fists, he could best any two average men in a fight. No doubt about it, Bass Reeves was the real deal.

I began writing the Buffalo Soldier series because, like many Americans my age, I grew up watching westerns on our old black and white TV or from the balcony in our town's segregated movie theater. It was only after joining the army in 1962 that I learned that the Wild West wasn't as lily white as I'd seen it portrayed in the movies and TV shows I'd seen. I learned, for example, that one in four of the cowboys on cattle drives or working ranches, was African-American, that ten percent of the U.S. army stationed west of the Mississippi between 1875 and 1900 were African-American. As a young private, I was assigned to the army's 24th Infantry Division in Augsburg, Germany. In the unit library I learned that the 24th traced its lineage back to the 24th Infantry Regiment, one of four units authorized by the U.S. Congress in 1875, that were staffed by black men and led by white officers. The others were the 25th Infantry, and the Ninth and Tenth Cavalry Regiments. After I left the army, I became a diplomat, and as I traveled the world representing the United States, I learned that more of the things I'd been exposed to in history classes, or in my consumption of popular media were wrong. The contributions of minorities and women were either mentioned only in passing, or completely omitted. That motivated me to start the series on the Buffalo Soldiers. Upon learning about Bass Reeves, I decided that I just had to write about this missing chapter in U.S. history

The problem, though, was that Reeves could neither read nor write English, so there exist no primary documents by him. One has to rely on second and third hand accounts; newspaper reports and comments about him by others in their journals and memoirs. Some of it is contradictory or far-fetched. For example, different sources list Reeves as born in Arkansas or in Texas. The weight of evidence tends to support Arkansas as his birthplace, but you can see the problem. A straight forward historical account would be difficult because of the lack of authoritative source material.

That left one thing – fiction. So, as I'd done with the Buffalo Soldiers, I did a ton of research, made tons of notes, and set out to write a fictionalized—but historically accurate—account of the life of Bass Reeves. I decided to focus primarily on his time as a deputy U.S. marshal. He'd been one of several African-Americans hired as deputies after Isaac Parker was appointed the U.S. Judge for the Western District of Arkansas and Indian Territory in 1875. Parker's belief was that these black men would be able to work more effectively with the tribes in the territory than white deputies. Bass Reeves worked as a deputy marshal for nearly 30 years, leaving that job only when the federal government dropped its efforts to build an inclusive society and focus on economic development. Post-Civil War reconstruction ended, and the era of Jim Crow began. Bass, along with other blacks, was fired from the marshal's service in the early 1900s. He was living in Muscogee, Oklahoma at the time, and was hired as a policeman. He served in that capacity until he died. Lauded for his services at the time, after the early 1900 shift in attitude, he was largely forgotten. He died and was buried in Muscogee, but currently, no one knows the exact location of his grave. Pretty hard to write an effective history under those circumstances.

Thus, *Frontier Justice: Bass Reeves, Deputy U.S. Marshal* was born. I was pleasantly surprised when the book began drawing attention and a readership. It seemed that people were interested in this forgotten figure. That was that, for a while. Then, I met J.C. Hulsey, of Outlaws Publishing, and host of an on-line radio show on the western genre, who had read the book and wanted to interview me about it. This led to me writing a number of novelettes about Bass Reeves, which were published by Outlaws.

The Old Cowboy, as J.C. is fondly known, decided to finally hang up his spurs, and Outlaws Publishing went out of business, taking the Bass Reeves books and several others off the market. My friend Nick Wales, a UK-based expert on westerns and book promotion, who is associated with DS Productions, which now publishes my western books, agreed that pulling these novelettes into a series of anthologies was a good idea, and since *Frontier Justice* was the book that started it all, it made since to launch the anthology series the same way.

So, here it is. *Bass Reeves: The Indomitable Lawman.* The first three stories, *Bass and the Preacher, The Marshal and the Madam,* and *Renegade Roundup* are very different. The first is entirely fictional, based on the fact that not much is known of Bass's stay in Indian Territory, so it's plausible that he might have met an itinerant preacher during his time there. The second is based on his relationship with the infamous outlaw, Belle Starr, which is borne out by historical accounts. The third is loosely based on stories of how Bass often brought in more than 10 fugitives at a time after one of his trips to the territory. Did things happen exactly as I outline in the story? I doubt it, but since there are no contemporaneous accounts, I figure my version is as good as any.

This is being done for Bass Reeves fan, past, present, and future. Keep your eyes open for the rest, and let me know what you think.

Bass and the Preacher

1.

His dark skin was slick with sweat, and grit from the red and brown dirt he'd been running across filled every crevice and orifice of his body. His breath came in ragged gasps, as much from fear as the exertion of legging it across miles of unfamiliar territory, all the time, glancing over his shoulder to see if the slave catchers were on his tail.

The July heat, just north of the town of Denison, Texas, and, if he remembered correctly the map he'd seen in his master's tent, about two miles south of the Red River, bore down on him like a thick wool blanket. Even the wind felt hot on his skin.

He'd been running for two days, and now, just a day shy of his twenty-third birthday, freedom was within his grasp. He only had to evade the slave catchers long enough to cross the river into Indian Territory, where he hoped he'd be able to hide out among the tribes he'd heard welcomed runaway slaves.

But, despite his youth and his excellent physical condition, Bass Reeves was tired, bone-tired like he'd never been before in his life. Tired or not, though, he knew that if he quit and was caught, he'd be lucky just to get a few lashes. The fact that he'd run away from an officer in the rebel army, or as his master, Colonel George R. Reeves, called it, the Army of the Southern States of the Confederacy. At any rate, even though he was a slave, he'd probably be treated like a deserter, only, unlike the whites who deserted, they probably wouldn't shoot him. No, for him, it'd be a short dance at the end of an even shorter rope—after a lashing that would flay the hide from his back.

So, tired or not, he'd keep running.

Avoiding roads and well-traveled trails, he ran through the pine forests, through thick forests of oak, birch, hickory, and pecan, through marshes thick with sedge and sawgrass, looking over his shoulder every few steps, always fearing that a band of slave catchers would come around the corner and be upon him at any moment.

When he made it to a small grove of willows on the banks of the river and saw no one behind him and no one on the other bank, he almost cried. All he had to do was find a place shallow enough to cross and he'd be free. After what felt like an eternity, but in reality, had only been five days, freedom was finally in sight.

Finding that place took almost an hour, but finally, wet up to his massive chest, and so tired he could barely put one foot in front of the other, he was in Indian Territory.

Just to be on the safe side, he walked north for another hour until he was deep within the rolling hills and thick forests. Now that his fear of slave catchers was lessened, he noticed that his stomach was growling. He'd not had time to steal much food before fleeing the rebel camp, only a few pieces of hardtack and a canteen of water. He'd been lucky to find several streams along the way, but the hardtack was gone by the third day. He was now into his second day of nothing but water and the occasional handful of black berries or hickory nuts. His stomach felt like it wanted to claw through his skin and eat his frayed leather belt.

But, he knew that he had to be well away from the river to stay free.

He eventually found a little clearing in the woods well away from any trails, and unlikely to be stumbled upon by the slavers., He made himself a bed of pine needles under a chinaberry tree and lay down. As hungry as he was, his body needed rest even more than food. He was asleep almost before his head hit the ground.

The smell of wood burning awakened him. Groggy at first, he forgot where he was. Then, when he remembered, panic struck.

His vision, as it often was when he first awoke, was fuzzy. But, he could see the flickering flames of a fire, and a dark figure near the fire. He rubbed his eyes, until he could see clearly, and couldn't believe what he was seeing.

A man, a skinny, and from the length of his legs, tall white man crouched next to a small fire, with his back to him, watching an iron coffee pot suspended over the flames.

As quietly as he could, he slid the Bowie knife, the only weapon George Reeves allowed him to have, from the sheath strapped to his ankle, and rose to a crouch.

The man at the fire, as if he had eyes in the back of his head, turned and looked at him, a broad smile on his narrow face.

"Well, pilgrim, I see you finally decided to come back from the Land of Nod and join the wide awake. How do you like your coffee?"

2.

The man was skinny, as skinny as a fence post. The once black, now dark gray with age and many harsh washings, broadcloth jacket he wore had a patch at the left elbow, and his pants were shiny at the knees and frayed at the cuffs. The planter's hat he wore squarely on his head, had once been white, but was now a dingy gray, and his linen shirt lacked collar and was a yellowish-brown from too many washings with lye soap.

Bass saw no sign of a sidearm but couldn't be sure he didn't have a pocket pistol, which was just as deadly as a rifle or a large caliber handgun up close. At that point, he decided that he'd rather be dead than return to slavery. He stood slowly, holding the knife low with the tip of the blade pointing at the stranger's gut.

"I ain't goin' back," he said. "You jest gon' have to kill me here."

The man slowly came up out of his crouched position, still having to look up at Bass's six-foot-two and held his empty hands out.

"I don't know where it is you don't want to go back to, pilgrim, but rest assured I have no intention of killin' you, or anybody else for that matter."

Bass stared intently at the man. While he could neither read nor write, he'd learned in his short life to read people, and he sensed that the man was telling the truth. But, he'd never before met a white man who talked like this one did.

"You mean to say you ain't fixin' to turn me in to the slave patrol?"

The man's eyes widened and he frowned. "Turn you in to--, why no I would never do anything like that. Why would you even think such a thing?"

"Most white folk I know 'round these parts own slaves, and them that don't support them that do."

"Well you just met one white person who neither owns slaves nor supports those who do." He bowed slightly at the waist. "Ebeneezer Cratchett at your service. Actually, Reverend Ebeneezer Cratchett."

Now, it was Bass's turn to look surprised. "You a preacher man?"

"I am," Cratchett said. "I'm here in Injun Territory to bring the Lord's words and blessings to the heathens."

"You got yourself a church somewhere?"

"For where two or three are gathered together in my name, there am I in the midst of them. Matthew 18.20. My church is anywhere people are willin' to sit and listen."

"Oh, you one of them circuit ridin' preachers. I seen 'em a time or two back in Arkansas, 'fore old man Reeves moved his family down to Texas. He wouldn't never 'low 'em to preach to us slaves. Said it'd give us high-falutin' ideas that'd just cause trouble. When he give me to his oldest son, George, and he done took off and joined the Texas militia, they wasn't too much on preachifyin' and such, 'cept for now 'n then, some jackleg preacher'd come by 'n rail agin' the Quakers 'n Methodists what was tryin' to ruin life for white folk in the south. Can't say I ever heard much to make me want to hear more."

"The words of Satan can be heard even in the church," Cratchett said. "Even from the mouths of those who call themselves men of God. Back home in Indianhead, Maryland, I heard such nonsense a lot, and it never did make no sense to me. So, I took to preachin' then. Never did no good, though. Them tobacco plantations was too dependent on slavery. I got run off more 'n one before I come to my senses and decided to head out here 'n try my luck at convertin' souls."

"You have much luck?"

"Not yet, but I ain't givin' up. Let us not become weary in doin' good, for at the proper time we will reap a harvest if we do not give up. That there verse is in Galatians. You oughta read your Bible, you'd see what I mean."

Bass looked downcast. "I can't read," he said. "Old man Reeves wouldn't 'low any of his slaves to learn to read or write. Said we didn't know how to read to work the fields or drive a buggy."

Cratchett smiled broadly. "Well, now, pilgrim, it 'pears my patience done rewarded me. You don't know your Bible, and I got me a feelin' you're a man in need of knowin' the truth. I think we oughta travel together for a spell, so's I can commence your education."

"I don' know, mister," Bass said. "I got me a long way to go, 'n I don' know if travelin' with you is such a good idea."

"Think about it, Bass. There are a lot of the slave patrols runnin' 'round the territory lookin' for runaways. A colored man travelin' all alone without . . . manumission papers . . ." Bass shook his head. "Well, without something provin' you're a free man you'd be fair game for any slave catcher, or anybody who wanted to collect the reward for turnin' in runaways. If you travel with me, I can introduce you to people as my manservant. That way ain't nobody gonna be askin' you for your papers."

Bass hadn't thought about that. He knew his journey would be perilous but had thought that once he got to Indian Territory, he would only have to dodge the patrols.

"I reckon that might not be a bad idea," Bass said. "We try it a few days 'n see how it work."

3.

For the rest of the day, the two men sat opposite each other at the fire Cratchett had built and shared their stories.

Cratchett started off by expanding on his life in the small town of Indianhead on the west shore of the Chesapeake Bay in Maryland, and how, even as a boy, he felt that the practice of holding other humans in bondage and treating sometimes no better than beasts of burden, as many of his neighbors who owned tobacco plantations did, was wrong. As he grew older he began speaking out against the practice, earning the enmity of nearly everyone in his community.

"You see," he said. "I was raised a Methodist, and from as far back as I can remember, I was taught to follow the teachings of John Wesley, our founder. He felt that slavery was wrong, and when the church was founded in Baltimore, Maryland, when this country was still young, Methodists were against slavery. Hell fire, they sent people all over the place urging people to free their slaves."

"Don't reckon they had much luck with that message," Bass said.

"Unfortunately, my young friend, you're right. Money talks, and cotton and tobacco was the main crops in the south, and they needed a large labor force to make money off it. Slaves was cheap labor. Now, the church, sad to say, ain't immune from the lure of money, so, in order to keep the money flowin' into the collection plates on Sunday mornin', the Methodists in the South started accomodatin' the planters. Along with the Baptists, they even tried to say that the Bible was okay with slavery as long as slaves were treated proper." He made a snorting sound. "I'll tell you, it don't do no such thing. They just changed the meanin' to make money."

Bass nodded. "I allus wondered how ole Massa Reeves could go to church on a Sunday mornin', 'n come back to a place where he was treatin' folk like property. So, the Bible don't say slavery is okay?"

"Not the way they say it. Anyway, I couldn't take it no more, so about five year ago, when I was thirty, I picked up and headed west. Stopped at a lot of places along the way, until I heard about Injun Territory, where they sent the Injuns when they stole their land back east. Figured this would be a good place to spread the true word, you know."

"Ain't many white folk like you," Bass said. "Least ways, none that I done met."

"There are more than you think, but in the South, it can be dangerous to hold such views, so they keep quiet. What about you, though, Bass? What's your story?"

Bass told him about being born on a plantation in Arkansas and being named Bass for his grandfather who he never knew. Because of his size and strength, his owner had taken him out of the field when he was still a boy, and made him his buggy driver, bodyguard, and companion.

"He took me ever where with him," he said. "Him and the other plantation owners used to talk 'bout stuff where I could hear, but they never paid me no mind. It was like I was a piece of furniture."

"Sounds to me like he trusted you a lot."

"I suppose. 'Ceptin' for not lettin' me learn to read or write, he treated me good enough. But, when he give me to his boy, George, it was different. Old George didn't whip me or nuthin', but he wasn't near as decent to me as his pappy was. He done joined up with the Texas militia when the war started, and he took me out to the battles 'n didn't even let me have a gun. That's when I decided to run away. I got tired of seein' men gittin' kilt."

Cratchett peered at Bass through the haze of smoke drifting up from the fire.

"You are a big 'un, Bass, I tell you that. You always been big like this?"

"Long's I can remember. I guess I'se jest born big. My bein' big's why ole man Reeves done picked me to be his bodyguard."

"You know, I'm no fortune teller, but I got this feelin' deep down inside my gut that you got a whole pack of adventure waitin' for you in this life, Bass Reeves."

Bass lifted the tin cup Cratchett had given him and took a sip of the chicory-flavored coffee. He peered at Cratchett over the rim of the cup.

"I ain't lookin' for adventure," he said. "All I want is to live peaceable and be left alone. I figure up here 'mongst the Injuns I can do that."

Cratchett waggled a finger at him.

"You have a lot to learn about the territory, my young friend," he said. "For instance, as a runaway, you'll want to be real careful with some of the Injuns, especially the Cherokee."

Bass looked at him, puzzled.

"Why I have to do that?"

"Well, there are a lot of tribes here, and they're all different. You got some, like the Cheyenne, and the Apache that just want to be left alone. The Choctaw ain't too bad most of the time. But, the Cherokee, well, they were slaveholders in their old lands, 'n they brought that practice to the territory when they were displaced. Most of 'the tribes done signed treaties with the South in the war, too, but I hear one faction of the Cherokee done formed a regiment to fight for the South, so if you run into a bunch of Cherokee, you're likely to be either enslaved or turned over as a runaway."

Bass shook his head. There was much about this place he had to learn. Maybe the preacher would be good for more than just covering his lack of freedom papers.

"Well, I 'spect I got a lot to learn, preacher man," he said. "So, I reckon you better start teachin'."

4.

Bass's education in the ways of Indian Territory continued each day for three days as the two men made toward the northwest, traveling through the southwest part of Choctaw land into the Chickasaw Nation. They avoided well-traveled trails, and made camp each night well inside the trees, often not building a fire in order to avoid being spotted.

On the second day of walking, for Cratchett had, he confessed to Bass, lost his horse in a card game in Muscogee the month before and had been afoot since, they were sitting on a rock on the bank of a meandering stream, soaking their aching feet in the cool water.

"Say," Bass said. "Whyn't you teach me some readin' from that Bible of yours?"

"Uh, that presents somethin' of a problem." Cratchett said. "You see, when I lost my horse, I also lost my saddlebags and all their contents, among which was the good book."

"So, how you know all them Bible verses you allus spoutin'?"

"Oh, I remember them. I have a good memory, you see."

Bass nodded. "Yeah, reckon I can understand that. I'm pretty fair at 'memberin' myself."

No more was said about reading lessons, as they put their boots back on and continued walking. Bass just felt lucky to have someone to talk to.

On the third day, though, their luck ran out.

They came over a little rise, and looked down into a peaceful green valley, dotted with pines, oaks, maples, and chestnuts, with a narrow stream running through it like a long, thin snake. Like two children, they whooped and hollered as they ran down the gentle slope, threw themselves down and plunged their heads into the chilled waters and lapped like thirsty horses.

They'd just come up for air the second time, when Bass stiffened and looked back up the slope.

"What is it?" Cratchett asked.

"I hear horses," Bass said.

Cratchett looked around. So did Bass. They were in the middle of a large clearing, with nothing higher than a few clumps of brush that didn't even come up to their knees. No place to hide.

"We should make a run for it?" Cratchett, wide-eyed, said.

"Ain't no place to run. We can't outrun a horse anyway."

Bass's voice was calm, but inside he was roiling with fear.

He felt an icy stab in his gut when he saw the first rider top the hill.

And, he was followed by another, and another, and another. Four men, even from a distance, Bass could see that they had the disreputable look of the slave patrol; men who'd evaded military duty to deal with less dangerous targets, runaway slaves. He knew that they'd have shotguns or repeating rifles in scabbards attached to their saddles, and possibly bullwhips as well, and wouldn't hesitate to use either on a recalcitrant runaway. Maybe, he thought, if I fight, they'll kill me quick.

Beside him, he could feel Cratchett shaking like a willow tree in the wind.

"We got to stay calm," he said.

"What will we do?"

"Well," Bass said. "I reckon we gon' have to pretend I'se your slave, 'n hope they believes it."

Cratchett looked wide-eyed at him. "You sure you can do this?"

"I been a slave all my life. I think I knows how to act like one. The question is, can somebody like you, what never owned slaves, act like a slave owner?"

Cratchett had an uncertain look on his face.

"If you can't do it," Bass said, with a note of desperation in his voice. "We's both likely gon' get ourselves kilt."

Cratchett took a deep breath.

"Then, I reckon we got no choice."

They stood as the riders approached, Bass a step behind Cratchett as he would do if he were in fact the man's slave. He kept his head bowed, but strained his eyes upwards to watch the men.

"Good day, gentlemen," Cratchett said when the four horsemen stopped about ten feet from them. "Fine day we're having, is it not?"

The man on the left, broad shouldered, but slightly hunch backed, with an unkempt black beard and a slouch hat that had once been brown, but was now smudged almost black, glared down at them.

"Howdy, yerself, mister," he said. "What y'all doin' way out here with no horse?"

"I had a run of bad cards and unfortunately, my horse and gear are now in someone else's possession," Cratchett said.

The man pointed at Bass. "What about this boy here? He b'long to ya?"

"Yes, this is my man servant. I would never risk him in a card game."

"Wha's yo name, boy?"

Before Bass could respond, Cratchett. "I don't allow him to speak to anyone without my express permission. His name's Benjamin."

Bass let out a breath, and said a silent prayer of thanks for Cratchett's ability to think so quickly.

"That ain't a bad idea. Got to keep these slaves in they place. He's a big 'un, though, to jest be a man servant."

"Uh, well, he's also my bodyguard."

At this, the man's eyes narrowed.

"You ain't give him no shootin' iron, have you? Folks 'round these parts don't cotton to slaves havin' weapons."

"Oh no, I'd never do that," Cratchett said. "His size and demeanor alone are usually enough to deter anyone with hostile intent."

"D'meanor? He ain't one of them uppity nigrahs, is he?"

"No, not at all. Benjamin's actually as gentle as a lamb. But, when he frowns, with his size, it has a chillin' effect on most people."

The man laughed. "Yeah, reckon I kin see that. You best tell 'im not to be frownin' at me, though, 'cause if he do, I'll put lead in that black hide of his."

"Why, sir, he'd never do that. After all, you gentlemen do not appear threatening, right, Benjamin?"

"Yassuh, massa," Bass said, ducking his head and smiling.

"You sure nuff got him trained all good and proper, mister. Well, we'll be on our way. We're on the trail of a slave what run away from his master down Texas way, a big, mean blackamoor. You be on the lookout for 'im. They's a big reward to the man what turns him in."

"I'll do that, sir, I surely will. I could use the funds at the moment, being kind of strapped as it were."

The four men laughed, and at their leader's signal, wheeled their horses and rode off toward the north.

Bass and Cratchett stood quietly watching until they were out of sight. When the dust from their horses was almost settled, Cratchett sighed loudly and wiped the sweat from his forehead. Bass let out a breath and stood to his full height, a half-smile on his face.

"You pretty good at this play actin'," he said.

"When one's life is on the line, my young friend, one finds the ability to do what's needed. Now, I believe it would be in our best interests to depart this area post haste."

"Which way we gon' go? I'se plannin' to head north, but that's the way they done gone, so I don' think it's such a good idea, but I for sure ain't gon' go back south."

"Well, I know I told you that the Cherokee can't be trusted, but northeast toward the Cherokee Nation's our best route for the moment. Once we put enough distance between ourselves and that band of ruffians, we can change course."

Bass shrugged. He couldn't come up with a better plan, so for the moment, at least, he would continue to follow the preacher.

5.

The next three days passed without incident. They took a meandering trail along the border between the Choctaw and Chickasaw Nations, heading, Cratchett informed Bass, toward the Creek lands and the settlement of Muscogee. He told him that this would hopefully help them to avoid entering the Cherokee Nation, as they should be able to head north by northwest up through Osage territory and cross into Kansas, where, hopefully, Bass would be able to evade slave patrols and rebel military units and make it to Canada and freedom.

Other than the tales he'd heard about following the North Star, Bass had no idea where he was, or what lay ahead, and found himself more and more dependent on the preacher's knowledge of the territory, a situation that bothered him immensely.

Bass passed the time by asking Cratchett questions about life in the territory, its history and inhabitants, and cataloguing the nature of the terrain, which had changed as they ventured farther north. Gone were the pines, chinaberry trees and generally flat terrain, replaced by thick stands of hardwoods, evergreens that he didn't recognize, and more tree-covered hills than he'd seen since leaving Arkansas as a boy for the trip to the flat and featureless terrain of the Reeves' new home in Texas.

They stayed off the well-traveled trails, and as a consequence saw few people. Those they did see, they avoided.

Then, one day, as the sun was sinking low, they decided to make camp beside a bubbling brook that flowed down from a particularly high hill to their north. Since they hadn't seen another soul all day, it was decided that it might be safe to build a fire to ward off the chill of night, which seemed much colder than it actually was because of the contrast with the heat of the day that pressed down on them like a heavy wool blanket.

Bass was enjoying himself, probably for the first time in a long time, sitting by the crackling fire, sipping coffee and eating some of the dried jerky Cratchett had been lucky enough to keep in a bag in his coat rather than his saddlebags. The sky was changing colors in a way that Bass particularly liked; a light touch of orange and pink near the horizon, turning darker until directly overhead it was already turning purple.

He was beginning to think that he would actually make it. Then, disaster struck.

Disaster came in the form of two scruffy looking white men with derby hats barely containing their stringy hair, more gum than teeth showing when they opened their mouths, and an odor that he detected even before they stepped out of the bushes upstream about twenty feet with the business ends of Colt .45 caliber Peacemakers pointing at him and Cratchett.

"Evenin' gen'lmen," the taller of the two, who was still a foot shorter than Bass, said. "It sure is a fine even', ain't it?"

Except for the movement of his head as he turned it toward the sound of the man's voice, Bass remained still. Cratchett, though, jumped sideways and almost tumbled into the fire.

"W-what, where'd you two come from," he said. "Why are you pointing those guns at us?"

"Well, it's like this," the other man said. "We kinda short on cash right now, 'n we've thinkin' on relievin' you two of any valuables and cash ya might be luggin' 'round."

Bass looked at Cratchett. The man was quivering and seemed unable to focus his eyes. The glibness he'd shown when they met up with the slave hunters seemed to have fled.

"Uh, mister," he said. "We ain't got no money, 'n we ain't got nothin' valuable, neither. We'se jest a couple of poor people headin' north lookin' for work."

The two newcomers shared a look.

"Whatcha think, Lester? Ya think this boy's tellin' us the truth?" He poked his revolver in Bass's direction.

"Naw, Clem, I think this big buck's lyin' through his teeth." He walked up to Cratchett and put the end of his Peacemaker's barrel against the preacher's nose. "Ain't that right, mister? Ain't he lyin'? Why ya let this boy talk fer ya, anyway?"

Cratchett stared cross-eyed at the pistol barrel. "N-no, he's not lyin'. I'm just an itinerant preacher, makin' my way through the territory to bring the word from the good Book to the heathens."

Both outlaws focused their attention on Cratchett, ignoring Bass.

"Is that a fact, now? Ya really a preacher man?" Clem asked. "Where ya got your church?"

"Clem," Lester said. "Ya ain't too smart. The man said he's a eye-ten-uh-runt. That means he move 'round all the time. Preacher like that ain't got no church."

Cratchett's head bobbed up and down. "That is correct, sir. I sometimes hold services under any convenient tree, in barns, any place people will gather to listen to me."

That seemed to amuse them. The two men laughed and slapped their thighs, but still kept a weapon trained on Cratchett.

"Thas good to hear, preacher," Clem said. "I been to church once't, 'n iffen I 'member correctly, the preacher took up a collection after he preached. Ya do that, preacher?"

"Uh, sometimes."

"Well, that mean ya oughta have some coin in your

pocket. Pass 'em over."

"I'm sorry, gentlemen, but I lost my money in the last town I passed through, along with my horse and all my supplies."

"Now, it ain't proper fer a preacher man to be lyin'," Lester said. "Now, ya gonna hand over the money, or do we have to git a mite rough with ya?"

"There is no need for rough-housing," Cratchett said. "I'll be happy to turn my pockets out so you can see that I have nothing of value."

Lester pushed the .45 harder against Cratchett's nose. "Well, what ya waitin' fer? Git to turnin' them pockets out."

The outlaws, in messing with Cratchett, had completely forgotten Bass, allowing him to sidle around until he was behind them. They didn't notice his move until large hands grabbed each of them by the shoulder, lifted them several inches off the ground, and slammed them against each other. Their heads collided with a dull thud, and their eyes rolled back in the sockets.

Bass held the two limp outlaws for a few seconds, looking at them like he would a water snake. Then he loosened his grip and let them flop to the dirt, where they lay sprawled out. Cratchett looked wide-eyed at him.

"My God, man," he said. "You are strong. I've never seen anyone who could do that."

"I done done a lotta liftin' and totin' in my life," Bass said. "These two don' weigh much more 'n a bag of cotton."

"Looks like they'll be out for a spell. They're gonna have terrible headaches when they wake up."

"Which reminds me," Bass said. "We'd best be makin' tracks fo they wakes up."

"That, my friend, is a capital idea." Cratchett began kicking dirt into the fire.

Bass knelt beside the two unconscious would-be

robbers and began undoing their gun belts.

"What are you doin', Bass?"

"They wakes up, they likely to come after us. Don' want 'em to be able to shoot us, do you? 'Sides, we kin use these to protect ourselves agin' night critters."

He picked the Peacemakers off the ground, blew the dust off and replaced them in their holsters. He held one out to Cratchett.

"No, thank you, my friend. I do not hold with such things. I never learned how to shoot. You keep them both."

Bass shrugged and stood. After putting both belts around his waist, let out to almost the last hole to accommodate his girth, he turned to face Cratchett.

"Well, how do I look?" he asked.

Cratchett smiled. "Like a deadly gunfighter. But, how come you got them pistols with the butts forward like that?"

Bass looked down at the two Peacemakers, their butts facing the front. "I don' know. It just seem like it'd be easier to git 'em out iffen I needs to this way."

Cratchett shrugged, and continued to gather their meager belongings. Bass knelt again and tugged off each man's boots.

"Why are you taking their boots?"

"Make it harder for 'em to follow us," Bass said. "I reckon they got horses hid somewhere 'round here, so we'll take them too."

Now, Cratchett laughed aloud.

"You know, Bass," he said. "When I first met you, despite your size, you seemed like the gentlest of souls. Now, though, I can see that you have a bit of larceny in your nature. It is dangerous to cross you."

Bass nodded. "I ain't never gone lookin' fer trouble, and I don' like hurtin' nothin', man or beast. But, I don' like people messin' with me, thas fo sure."

6.

They found the robbers' horses tied to a chinquapin tree less than two hundred yards from their camp. After they'd untied the two horses, a large white stallion that shied when Cratchett approached, but seemed to like Bass, and a roan with a gentle disposition, Bass tossed the outlaws' boots into the sage growing near the tree. They turned the horses' noses due north and kicked their flanks with the aim of putting as much distance between themselves and the two as they could before they woke up from the head-knocking Bass had administered.

The white stallion was one of the finest horses Bass had ever seen in his life, better even than the horses William Reeves raised, and he seemed to welcome Bass upon his back. As they rode away, Cratchett cling to his saddle horn with a fearful look on his face, Bass sat with his back straight and his head erect. He rode tall in the saddle.

They rode at an easy canter for two hours, covering about twelve miles. Cratchett looked like he was ready to fall from the saddle.

"Ya want to stop for a while?" Bass asked. "I reckon we'se far enough away them fellas can't catch up to us, 'specially since they ain't got no boots."

Cratchett pulled the roan to a jerky stop. "A bit of rest would not be unappreciated."

Slowly, like an old man with arthritis, he dismounted. Bass stopped the stallion and slid off his back with a practiced move.

"Ya know, I could use somethin' to eat, too," Bass said. "My gut's a'tryin' to claw it's way through my skin."

Cratchett opened his bag and peered inside.

"I'm afraid all we have left is a can of beans and a bit of hard tack."

"Sho could use some meat with them beans 'n bread. I think I'll go hunt me up some jack rabbit."

"How in blazes do you expect to catch a rabbit?"

Bass patted the Colts at his waist.

"I reckon these here .45's will work jest fine."

As he turned to walk into the surrounding brush, he saw a flash of brown about thirty feet away in a patch of berry vines.

"Well now, looks like the good Lord done answered my prayer and provided," he said.

Cratchett gave him a funny look, a look that turned to amazement as Bass's right hand moved so fast it was blur. One minute his hand was empty, and the next he was raising, cocking, and firing the Peacemaker. There was a bang, a flash of flame from the barrel, and a small cloud of smoke. Cratchett jumped at the sound. Bass jumped up and down and shouted gleefully.

"Got 'im," he said. "We'se gon' have us some stewed rabbit for supper."

"Rabbit? What rabbit?"

Cratchett looked confused as Bass ran to the berry bush and knelt. He looked amazed when he reached in and when he withdrew hand, he was holding a rather large rabbit, with the top of its head and one ear gone from the impact of the .45 caliber slug Bass had put in it.

"Wha-, how, I didn't even see that animal," he said. "How'd you hit it from that far away?"

"Aw, this was an easy shot. Ole man Reeves wouldn't let me learn to read 'n write, but when he seen I had a sharp eye, he let me learn how to shoot a rifle and a pistol. Said I'd need it to be his bodyguard. Plus, he used to enter me in the turkey shoots. Fo I'se fifteen I could outshoot any man for miles around. Won most of them shootin' competitions, I did."

Cratchett stood there rubbing at his sore hindquarters and looking at Bass, his expression one of naked astonishment. "Wait a minute. You tellin' me that man wouldn't let you learn to read or write, but he let you have a gun?"

"Well, only when he was around, and I had to give it back to him when I was done a'shootin' in them turkey shoots. Once or twice he even let me keep a couple of bits outa the purse I done won."

"That, my friend, is precisely why I so abhor slavery." Cratchett shook his head. "It not only debases the slave, but the master as well."

"I don't understand what you mean by debase."

"It means that you are treated as less than human. In the eyes of the man who claims ownership of you, you are not a man, but a unit of economy, no different than a horse or a wagon."

Bass chuckled. "I reckon you right, and I ain't never gon' let nobody treat me like that again. But, I did get somethin' outa it."

"Yeah, what?"

"I learned how to shoot pistol or rifle with either hand, 'n I reckon I kin outshoot any man within a hundred mile. Now I got me some shootin' irons, anybody think I ain't a man jest as good as he is, gon' be in fo a big surprise."

"I think, Bass Reeves, that you are right on that. Say, this looks like as good a place as any to set up camp. I'll get a fire started if you'll skin that rabbit."

7.

The next day, they resumed their journey, covering much more ground now that they had horses. By late afternoon they had passed through the Seminole lands and were well into Muscogee territory. They'd come to a place where several trails intersected, some of them, from the number of hoof and wheel prints, heavily used.

"I don't think it's a good idea to camp around here," Caldecott said. "Too much chance of someone coming along and spotting us."

"I suppose you right," Bass said. "Which way you think we oughta go?"

"Well, if we keep on our present course, we'll be in the Cherokee Nation tomorrow night, next day at the latest, but if we turn a bit more north, we'd be going through Osage territory. We'd get there in about two days travel, I think."

Bass was scanning the many hoof marks as he listened to Caldecott talk.

"Sho is a lot of Injuns up here," he said. "I didn't know they was so many tribes all in one place."

"Yeah, and only a hand full of the ones currently here are original inhabitants. The government in Washington looked at the land out here as a place to settle the Injuns from back east after they kicked them off their land ever since they bought the Louisiana territory from the French. Old Andy Jackson, Injun hater that he was, kicked it up a notch when he was president, so tribes from east, west, north, and south of here been kicked off their traditional tribal lands and moved here. Up in the northeast of the Cherokee Nation, there's a little chunk of land, they got nearly ten different tribes living on."

Cratchett stopped talking as Bass dismounted and

went to his knees.

"What's the matter? What're you looking at?" he asked.

Bass pointed to an area covered in a confusing mix of hoof prints.

"Them slave catchers done rode through here, 'n they's headin' right in the direction you want us to go."

Cratchett's brow wrinkled in confusion.

"How do you know that?"

"When they come up on us before, I noticed one of they horses had a nick in one of his shoes. That same horse passed here, headin' the same way you want us to go, 'n it wasn't too long ago."

Cratchett dismounted and knelt near Bass. Even peering hard, he was unable to see what Bass was talking about until the big man hovered a finger directly over the track in question.

"Dang, Bass, you got one sharp pair of eyes," he said. "And, the fact you even noticed that in the first place and remembered it all this time is amazing."

"I allus had a good memory. When you can't read, 'memberin' things is important. Noticin' things is important too. Man what don't pay no mind to where he put his foot's liable to step on a rattlesnake."

"Hm, there's a whole lot of truth in that, Bass, a lot." Cratchett frowned. "But, this puts a hitch in our plan to head up to Osage territory. It'd be hard to dodge them slavers up there."

Bass pointed west. "Why can't we head thataway?"

"Fort Sill's off to the west. Bound to be rebel soldiers out that way. Same thing to the east, 'n you know what's south of us. No, we need to keep headin' north. Looks like our only choice is to go through the Cherokee Nation and take our chances."

"I thought you said them Cherokee was slavers, too."

"They are, and that's a good reason for going that way," Cratchett said. "First of all, that slave patrol probably knows about the Cherokee, and they'll figure you'd never go that way. So, all we have to do is avoid the Cherokee."

Bass squinted in deep thought. It didn't make a lot of sense to him; going into the territory of a tribe that held slaves and that was sympathetic to the rebellious southern states. But, on the other hand, the preacher had a point. That would be the last place a slave patrol would think he'd go. Of course, riding through Cherokee territory and avoiding the Cherokee, seemed to him like walking through a thicket of brambles and expecting not to get scratched. He was in a quandary. Every course open to him seemed bad. Then, he shrugged. When nothing but bad choices are what you have, you take the least bad.

"Okay, preacher man," he said. "We go through Cherokee land."

8.

As they rode towards the northeast, the land began to slope upwards, and the cypress and evergreen forests of the south gave way to expanses of mostly post oak, elm, cedar, and pine, with oxbow lakes in many of the valleys. Cratchett, who knew the history of the region, was ignorant when it came to many of the plants and animals, so he was amazed at Bass's almost encyclopedic knowledge of such things. Bass seemed to know the name of every tree, which animals were easy to hunt and made good eating, and which to avoid, and read the weather expertly. This latter skill came in handy for a number of reasons. They were traveling during that time of year when the eastern part of Indian Territory was subjected to frequent tornados, and Bass seemed to know instinctively when a jumble of black clouds was about to spawn a deadly tail that would rip through the terrain, turning trees into matchsticks and tossing anything loose, like a man or a horse, around like tumbleweeds. They encountered two twisters during the first five days of their trek, but Bass was able each time to find a depression in which men and horses could ride out the storm, which usually only lasted a few minutes, but each time had left Cratchett shaking in his boots. The other was his knowledge of how to survive the temperature extremes common to the region. The days were hot and humid, sucking the energy right out of a body, but at night, it got cold enough to enable them to see the vapor from their breathing in the light from the camp fire. Bass knew the importance of pacing himself during the day, taking frequent rest breaks in whatever shade they could find and drinking plenty of water, and finding a sheltered spot at night and building a reflector of broken tree limbs, leaves and rocks for the fire at night to warm them as they slept.

Wary now of running into the slave catchers, their progress was considerable slower than it had been, covering no more than five or six miles per day.

"I'm powerfully sorry for us having to slow down like this," Cratchett said one day. "I know how much you want to make it to freedom."

"Ain't no need to 'pologize," Bass responded. "I'se free already, and ever day I wake up a free man, I thank God."

And, on they rode. Plunging deeper into the verdant green, but unknown territory before them.

Bass continued to amaze Cratchett with his ability not just to survive in the wild, but to thrive. Bass showed him how to weave cattails and milkweed and use small saplings to create a snare that caught small animals, and how to even use fragments of rabbit bone and convert these snares into efficient fish traps. Their eating improved day by day, as did their mood.

Then, one day, as they topped a rise, looking down into a lush green valley through which a wide stream meandered, Cratchett pulled his horse to a stumbling halt and hollered for Bass, who was riding a few feet ahead, to stop.

"What's the matter?" Bass asked, twisting in his saddle to look back. "Why we stoppin'? They's good clean water down there, 'n my throat's plumb parched."

"This is the border between the Muscogee lands and the Cherokee Nation, Bass," Cratchett said. "We need to think real careful before we go riding down there."

"Why? 'Cause the Cherokee done sided with the rebs? Ain't some of the other tribes done the same?"

"Well, yeah, many of the members of the so-called Five Civilized Tribes side with the southern cause, mostly because they're angry at the U.S. Government for forcin' them off their lands back east. But, the

Cherokee, before they left Tennessee and North Carolina had adopted slavery, copying their white neighbors in the hopes that it'd help their cause of keeping their lands. Of course, it didn't work. Old Andrew Jackson booted 'em off their land anyway. Just sayin', that of all the tribes supportin' the Confederate cause, the Cherokee are the ones you have to be real careful of."

Bass surveyed the land ahead. It looked so peaceful, it was hard for him to accept that it could hold the danger of re-enslavement.

"Well, I reckon I'se jest gon' have to take my chances," he said. "I fo sure ain't goin' back south. Iffen you worried, I'd understand if you parted ways with me right now."

Cratchett' frowned. He wagged a finger in Bass's direction. "Now, you listen up, my young friend. I promised I'd see you through Injun Territory, and I'm a man of my word. 'Sides, all them shootin' and trackin' skills you got won't do you a plug nickel worth of good if you run into a bunch of Johnny Reb Injuns."

"That mean you still gon' ride with me?" Bass cocked his head to the side.

"Of course, it means I'm still riding with you. What'd I just say?"

Bass laughed. "I'se just funnin' you, preacher man. I'm mighty happy to have your comp'ny. Now, can we ride on?"

9.

Luck seemed to be on their side. They rode northwest through the Cherokee Nation, hoping to reach Osage territory before encountering anyone. Luck, though, is a fickle mistress. One day, it's all roses, and the next, your hand's full of thorns.

Luck turned her back on them at mid-morning on the second day.

They had come down off a low ridge line, and were riding on a medium-wide path through a thick forest of post oak and pine. It had recently rained, and the ground underneath the dead leaves and pine needles was soft and cushiony. Easy on the horses, but it tended to deaden the sound of their hooves. The loudest sounds were an occasional whinny, the creaking of the saddle leather, the coo of mourning doves somewhere in the trees, and the whispering sound of the wind blowing through the leaves and needles.

Later, Bass would chide himself for his inattention. He didn't expect Cratchett to understand the need for constant vigilance, the same level of watchfulness that would be required if you were hunting bear, where letting mind wander off what you were there for could end up with the bear hunting you.

They were both surprised, but Bass was even more chagrined, when they rode around a blind turn in the trail and came face to face with twenty Cherokee soldiers; not the traditional Indian warriors that would make up a hunting or raiding party, but a group of real, honest to goodness soldiers. Some of them wore forage caps, and one or two even had on rebel gray tunics with gold braid on the shoulders. The man in charge was easy to spot. He rode a white horse that looked like the twin of the one Bass was riding, and wore a complete Confederate uniform, complete with a cockaded hat, and a sword dangling at his left side. At his side was another man in an almost-complete uniform carrying a long standard bearing a flag that at first Bass thought was the Stars and Stripes of the Union, until he looked closer and saw that it had only two red stripes flanking a white stripe upon which was stitched the words 'Cherokee Braves,' and the blue field had eleven white stars encircling five crossed stars.' He didn't need Cratchett to explain what the flag meant; the eleven white stars, he knew, represented the eleven states currently in rebellion, and having heard Cratchett's stories about the Five Civilized Tribes almost every day since they'd met, he figured they were represented by the five red stars.

They'd encountered a Cherokee rebel unit. He felt a cold stab in his gut when the leader of the Cherokee unit raised his hand, fearing the next sound he'd hear would be the crash of rifles. But, it turned out to be an order for the column to halt.

Bass and Cratchett stopped their horses.

The two groups, twenty armed Cherokee, and two men, only one with a weapon of any kind—and, Bass figured the two Peacemakers at his waist wouldn't stand a chance against nineteen Springfield rifles he could see strapped to each soldier's back—were stopped about twenty or twenty-five feet apart. He might get one or two before they brought him down, but this would be, he knew deep down in his soul, a one-sided battle. At twenty-five feet, he wouldn't miss, but he figured he wouldn't even get the chance to fire all six rounds in each weapon before one of the soldiers got lucky.

The leader of the Cherokee turned in the saddle and conferred with the man immediately behind him. Bass breathed a sigh of relief at the reprieve, and hoped it wouldn't come to a gun battle.

"Wonder what they're talkin' about," Cratchett said

in a quiet voice.

"Reckon we 'bout to find out," Bass said, pointing toward the two soldiers, the one the officer had spoken to and the standard bearer, walking their horses toward them.

Bass was careful to keep his hands resting on his saddle horn, not threatening in any way, but close enough that he could draw the Colts if needed.

The two soldiers stopped six feet from them. The standard bearer glared at them, but kept quiet.

"The captain would like to know what are you men doing here in the Cherokee Nation," the other man said.

"Why, I'm just an itinerant preacher lookin' for souls to save," Cratchett said. "My servant and I travel around offering to share the word of the Lord with those who would listen."

"You sure you are not a Yankee spy?"

"Why, listen to me speak, son. Do I not sound like a son of the South? Have I not my own personal slave and body servant to accompany me and take care of my personal needs?"

The soldier turned his attention to Bass. "What is your name, black man?"

Bass almost blurted out his real name, until he remembered what Cratchett had called him in front of the slave patrol. "My name's Benjamin," he said. "I b'long to Massa Cratchett."

"You know how to use those guns you're wearing?"

"Reckon I do. I have to protect Massa Cratchett. Can't do that iffen I can't use these here guns, now can I?"

The Indian stared at Bass, his eyes narrow slits. Finally, he made an 'hmph' sound and turned back to Cratchett.

"Where are you going, preacher?"

"I thought we might go up to the Cherokee Nation capital at Tahlequah, and then over to Osage Territory.

That is permissible, is it not?"

"Not many people left. John Ross and his people run off to Kansas, and the rest of the braves are joining the southern cause. Nothing left but a few children and old squaws. Been a lot of fighting in Tahlequah, so there's not much left of the town now."

"Well, now, the souls of women and children need saving, too, especially under the circumstances of this dreadful war," Cratchett said.

"Maybe you should go back down to the land of the Creek," the soldier said, spitting. "They are like old women and children. Their chief took his people and ran away to Kansas like the coward Ross. They are too afraid to fight."

"We just came through there, and didn't see many people. I think you're right. They must've all run away."

After a few more swinging glances between Cratchett and Bass, and back again, the soldier was apparently satisfied.

"Well, preacher, you be careful," he said. "Maybe you say a prayer to the Great Spirit for us so that we can kill many Yankee soldiers and those who follow them."

"I'll do just that, my good man. May God go with you."

The two soldiers turned and rode back to their formation. After a hushed conversation with the commander, they resumed their places in the formation, and the officer gave the command to move out.

Bass and Cratchett kept their horses still as the twenty men moved past them at a trot, several of them glancing furtively at them as they did. They waited until the soldiers were completely out of sight before resuming their journey, moving at a slow trot, only now, Bass kept his eyes and ears focused on the terrain ahead of them.

"I certainly hope that's the last we see of soldiers," Cratchett said.

"Ain't the soldiers that bother me," Bass said. "They seemed well-behaved, 'n not too interested in us. I'm prayin' we don't see no more slave patrols. You got a prayer for that, I'd appreciate if you'd say it."

10.

Despite the lack of hostility shown by the Cherokee unit they'd met, Bass and Cratchett mutually agreed that avoiding them was a good idea, so they stayed as far west in the Cherokee lands as possible. At one point, Bass had suggested turning west into Osage lands, and then bearing north, but Cratchett felt that given the fact that the Osage, a plains tribe that had been forced out of Kansas, had never been slave owners, and even though they'd signed a treaty with the Confederacy like the rest of the tribes, they were unlikely to cooperate with slave patrols, therefore, that was likely one of the first place the patrol would go looking for him. Bass wasn't totally convinced, but his ignorance of the territory left him no choice but to go along with the preacher.

Cratchett told him that hunting farther west wasn't nearly as good as it was in the heavily-wooded east, and the vegetation and ground cover was so sparse in places you couldn't hide a jack rabbit, whereas, in the east, the wooded valleys and deep forests offered a great number of hiding places.

The number of lakes and streams reminded Bass a bit of the plantation he'd lived on in Arkansas. One day, he thought, I'd like to go back there and do me some farming. He smiled at the thought. He was even thinking about taking a wife, and he had just the woman in mind. He'd first seen Nellie Jennie, a house servant for one of the wealthy white families in the Texas town William Reeves had moved his family to, and had even had the nerve to speak to her on one or two occasions. A tiny wisp of a woman, she was strong-willed, had a fine sense of humor, and, to Bass, was just about the most beautiful human being he'd ever seen in his life—and, that included his mother.

So, this is what freedom is. A man can have dreams, and have a chance to make them dreams come true. I can see now why so many people done run away to follow that North Star. Even out here, sleeping on the ground, eating nothin' but jack rabbits, fish, and beans, I feel like a great weight done been lifted off my back.

As he rode along, thinking about the future, but with a goodly part of his mind still on the terrain through which they passed, he began singing, *'I got one mo river ta cross, one mo mountain ta climb, one mo valley I got ta go through, to leave my troubles behind—"*

"What's that you're singing, Bass?" Cratchett asked.

"It's called, 'One Mo River to Cross'," Bass said. "When we slaves would be 'lowed to have church, it's one of the songs we sung. Ridin' through this land, it jest come to my mind."

Cratchett looked around at the rolling, tree-covered hills, crisscrossed by scores of streams, and nodded.

"Yes, it is quite appropriate. You'll have to teach it to me. I think it would be a good hymn to add to my services."

"I don' reckon I 'member all the words, but I teach you what I do 'member."

And, so, they rode on for the next hour, with Cratchett, despite his deep speaking voice, a voice that Bass could imagine delivering a rousing fire and brimstone sermon, singing off key. They sang 'One More River to Cross,' until Bass begged off because he could never remember the second and third verses, 'Swing Low Sweet Chariot,' which Caldecott knew, and 'Amazing Grace,' which brought tears to their eyes.

"You got a spirited singin' voice," Bass said when they decided to take a break from singing.

"I do love a good hymn. It lifts the spirit and makes the world seem a better place somehow."

Bass nodded. "It do that. But, I reckon thas the

whole reason for singin', ain't it? Lift up the spirit, 'n make things seem brighter. Trouble is, though, the old real world come a crashin' back in soon's you stop singin'."

"You do have a point, Bass, but you're much too young to have such a sour outlook on life."

"I might be young in years, preacher, but I'se old in spirit, and being taken to war, 'n watchin' men get blowed apart by grape shot 'n gutted with bayonets, done made that spirit even older."

Cratchett rubbed at his chin.

"Things like this do make one wonder, I will admit. How can a creature that's supposed to be created in God's image do such terrible things to his fellow creatures? It is a heavy question to ponder, so what say we find a place to camp and we can talk further on it."

Bass smiled. "That sounds like a good idea." He pointed. "That hill over yonder look like a good place to camp, 'n I bet we find some rabbits or squirrels in that bush that'd go jest fine with that last can of beans you got in that sack."

"I'd really like fish. Why can't we camp at the base of the hill?"

"The top of the hill's a better place 'cause we can see what's comin' at us from all directions," Bass said. "After runnin' into that buncha Cherokee soldiers, I ain't in the mood to take no chances."

Cratchett shrugged. "Well, rabbit it is. Maybe we can get fish tomorrow?"

"We see," Bass said, as he urged the stallion toward the hill.

Once they reached the top, Bass selected a flat expanse of ground under an oak tree, from which he had a clear view north, south, and west, and only had to move a few feet to see to the east. He snared a rabbit, skinned it, and soon had it on a spit over a fire Cratchett had built. Cratchett had also, while Bass worked on the rabbit, brewed a pot of coffee.

They sat at the fire, sipping the strong brew, while the rabbit sizzled.

"Hm," Cratchett said. "This was a good idea. We get a nice breeze up here, the air is fresh and clean, and that rabbit smells delicious."

Bass took a sip of the coffee. "Coffee ain't bad neither. 'Course, that nice breeze gon' be freezin' come nightfall."

"You are such a pessimist."

"Ain't no pessimist, I'se a Baptist," Bass said.

Cratchett laughed. "No, Bass, pessimism is not a religion—although, I think for some people it amounts to one—pessimism is having a negative view of life. Pessimists always see the bad side of things."

"That jest might be 'cause it's allus the bad side of things that come up on ya when you least expects it, and bites you in the hindquarters, don't ya think?"

"A pessimist you might be, but you do wax philosophical."

Bass's brow furrowed. "The only thing I done ever waxed was ridin' boots what didn't even belong ta me. That there rabbit's good 'n brown, I think it's callin' fer us ta eat."

Bass took the rabbit off the spit, and with his knife, split it lengthwise, giving half to Cratchett, while Cratchett shared out the last of the canned beans. They ate in silence.

Bass was gnawing the last bit of meat off the hind leg when he noticed a glint off in the distance. He stopped eating and focused on where he'd seen the quick flash of light. Before long, he could make out four riders making their way directly toward where he and Cratchett were sitting. He tossed the rabbit bones into the fire and crouched, looking intently, trying to estimate how far away the riders were.

"What's the matter, Bass?" Cratchett asked.

"We got comp'ny comin'. Four riders, 'n I'll bet you

my boots they's them slave catchers."

Cratchett's eyes widened.

"Good Lord, what are we gonna do?"

"We gon' git on our horses 'n git outa here as fast as we can, that's what we gon' do."

Cratchett, a man accustomed to moving at a slow pace, could, when the situation called for it, move quite rapidly, and that he did, stowing his eating utensils and getting his horse ready to travel almost as quickly as Bass did. They were mounted and ready to ride in less than two minutes.

But, mounted men can travel a great distance in two minutes, especially if their horses are moving at a gallop, which is what Bass could now see the approaching riders were doing. If he and Cratchett didn't move, he estimated that the riders would be upon them in less than five minutes.

"Which way we going?" Cratchett asked.

The west was out, as was the south, and north of them the terrain looked too rough for horses. They were left with only one choice; east, deeper into the Cherokee Nation. Bass pointed east and gently nudged the white stallion in the side.

The horse shot forward, going into a gallop in an instant. Cratchett hung on to the roan's main as he followed his friend.

They rode down the slope like men being pursued by the hounds from hell, leaving behind the ground that had been recently dampened by rain and entering a patch of land that was dry, causing their horses to kick up quite a cloud of dust. Bass didn't like making such an easy sign to trace, but consoled himself with the knowledge that their pursuers would have to travel over the same ground, thus also betraying their position. He leaned over the stallion's withers and silently prayed for a miracle.

11.

Had Bass been alone, he would've run his horse hard for an hour until he was in some deep woods, and then found a place to rest out of sight of the traveled trails until the horse was rested, and then he would've made a full-out run north. But, Cratchett had saved his hide on two occasions, at no small risk to himself, and even though Bass felt the man had an irritating habit of using big words that he didn't understand, he was one of the most decent white men he'd ever met in his life, and that included a few of the wrinkled old white preachers William Reeves had allowed to minister to his slaves, who talked about how the Bible told the servants to be obedient to their masters, and how the black folks had been cursed by God because Ham had laughed at the nakedness of his father, Noah. Hell fire, Bass thought, if he'd ever laughed at his papa, God wouldn't get a chance to curse him; the old man would've tanned his hide to a fare the well, and you can bet he'd never do a foolish thing like that again.

He enjoyed Cratchett's interpretation of the Good Book, because it was more in line with his own idea of God, a Being who was kind and caring, and who was willing to forgive the occasional lapse.

So, he couldn't abandon the preacher, even though it meant slowing his pace to allow the man to keep up. Every time he let the white stallion have his head and go into a full-out run, Cratchett would end up hanging off the side of his horse, tangled up in the reins and stirrups, because he was unable to stay seated at that speed.

Every so often, he'd take a gander over his shoulder at the thin cloud of dust being kicked up by their pursuers, and every time, it seemed to be getting closer.

He was at a loss for a way out of the mess he found himself in. His sense of honor and decency wouldn't allow him to just kick his horse into a run and let the hapless Cratchett fend for himself. He figured, he'd just have to try and fight his way out of it when the four riders caught up, and the way that cloud of dust was getting closer and closer, he felt pretty sure they'd catch up sooner rather than later.

At least, he thought, with the two Colts, both of which were fully loaded with .45 caliber slugs, with ten extra slugs on each belt, he stood a chance against only four men. They wouldn't expect him to be armed, and even if armed, they were probably arrogant like most slave chasers, and thought just the sight of an armed white man would cow a black man into submission.

They were in for a big surprise, he mused. Bass Reeves was one black man who was not about to submit to anything or anybody.

Suddenly, as he looked at the terrain ahead, he realized that things had gone from bad to really bad. They'd ridden into a canyon. The sides were too steep, and while the far wall was shallow enough to ride a horse up, he wouldn't be able to do it at a gallop, and he'd be wide open to a man with a rifle for the whole climb to the top. Not a good situation.

He pulled the stallion to a halt. Out of breath, and clutching the reins so hard his knuckles were white, Cratchett stopped beside him.

"W-why . . we s-stopping? They c-can't b-be far b-behind us," he said.

Bass pointed at the slope in front of them.

"We start up that slope, and we be like ducks in a tub, 'n ain't no way to git up the sides. We jest gon' have to stand 'n fight."

Cratchett's face, red from the exertion of hanging onto his horse, lost some of its color. "F-fight? There's four of them and you're the only one of us with a gun. I know you're a good shot, but can you take four men?"

"Guess I'm gon' find out," Bass said. He drew both Colts, checked the cylinders, and held them across the saddle horn, facing the oncoming cloud of dust.

The riders were still out of sight over the ridge they'd just crossed.

"We're dead men," Cratchett moaned.

"You can go on and hightail it outa here," Bass said. "I reckon they wants me, so they ain't likely to shoot at you. Go on, go up that hill, and git outa here."

Cratchett shook his head.

"N-no. I said I'd see you to safety. I'm not leaving."

Bass hoped that if he lost his fight with the four men, they'd at least let the preacher live. He was a good man who didn't deserve to die like this. He took a deep breath, and turned to face his pursuers.

"You sit there like that, and those men following you are likely to stand off and pick both of you off with their rifles," a voice said from a clump of small trees.

Bass's mouth dropped open and he spun around in the saddle, bringing both revolvers to bear on the man who stepped from the vegetation.

"W-where you come from?" Bass asked the swarthy man approaching them.

He wore denims, the preferred pants of cow hands, and a brown cotton shirt. His hair was long and held in place by a decorated head band, and his skin, a reddish-brown color, as dark as Bass's brown skin. An Indian, Bass thought, figuring he must be Cherokee since they were well inside the Cherokee Nation, but what was he doing out here alone. Bass noted that he carried one of the new Winchester repeating rifles, but wasn't holding it in a threatening manner.

"My name is Henry Lone Tree," the man said. "And, as you can see, I came from that clump of trees back there."

"What you doin' out here all by yourself?"

"That is not important, although, I could ask what the two of you are doing on Cherokee land, and why those four men are chasing you."

"They are a slave p-patrol," Cratchett said. "And they're after Bass here 'cause he ran away."

Lone Tree nodded. "I figured as much. They will be here soon, and even though you look like you know how to use those pistols you have, it would be best not to fight at all."

"Now, how I gon' do that? They ain't likely to listen iffen I offers to talk things out."

"No, that is true. But, if you are not here when they arrive, there will be no need for talking or fighting."

"Now, how I gon' do that? I ain't no magician."

"True," Lone Tree said. "But, I am. I can make you and the white man disappear."

12.

Henry Lone Tree wasn't a magician, really, but the way he'd hidden the entrance to a cave in the hillside, a cavern big enough to hold a stagecoach and team of horses, with an entrance Bass could ride his horse through and only have to bend a little, well, he was the next best thing to magic. Even with Bass's sharp eyes he hadn't seen it.

"Now, the two of you get on in there, and keep quiet," he said.

"What you gon' do 'bout them four men?" Bass asked.

"Do not worry. I will deal with them."

After Bass and Cratchett had entered the cave, Henry carefully replaced the cover of limbs he'd constructed, and stepped back to take a look. Satisfied that the cave entrance was once again invisible, he looked at the oncoming cloud of dust.

"Huh, they will be here soon. Guess I'd better get my dumb Injun act ready."

After brushing out the tracks of their horses with a limb he cut from one of the oaks, he gathered some twigs and small pieces of deadwood, and put them in a circle in a patch of dirt. Then, quickly, he withdrew a box of Lucifers, lit one, and set the pile of wood ablaze. By the time the four men arrived, he was seated, cross-legged before the fire, his arms folded across his chest, and his eyes closed.

The four men brought their horses to rattling halts six feet from him, sending a shower of dust and grit his way. He did not move or acknowledge their presence.

"Hey, Injun," one of the men said. "You see two men, a scruffy white man claimin' ta be a preacher and a big black buck, go by here?"

Henry continued to hold his head up and his eyes tightly closed.

"Say, Jeb," another man said. "You think mebbe this redskin's deaf or sump'in?"

"Mebbe he's one of them medicine men, and he's in a spirit trance," another said.

"Hell, y'all kin set here a jawin', I'm gonna find out," a fourth voice said. Its owner dismounted and walked to where Henry sat. "Hey, boy, did'ncha hear us talkin' to ya?"

He nudged Henry with the toe of his boot.

Henry opened his eyes and looked up at him.

"Who disturbs my spirit walk?" he said.

"Whatcha talkin' 'bout, Injun?" the man asked. "What the hell's a spirit walk?"

"I walk with my totem spirit, the wolf. Now, I must start my walk over from the beginning."

"Okay, Injun. I'm sorry I messed up yer walk. I jest need to ask ya a question, 'n we'll be on our way."

Henry sighed deeply.

"You white eyes are always in a hurry. What do you wish to ask me?"

"You didn't hear what Jeb asked you jest a minute ago?"

"When I am on the spirit walk, this world does not exist. I hear nothing, I see nothing. Now, what is your question?"

"You seen a white man and a colored boy come by here today?"

Henry closed his eyes again, and the man made a growling noise.

"Now, dammit, redskin, don't you start that spirit mumbo jumbo agin, ya hear. I wanna know iffen you seen a black buck and an old white man. They'd be ridin' a white stallion and a roan they done took from two wannabe robbers. We run inta them a ways back, 'n they said that black boy done stomped the both of 'em with his bare hands, 'n then the two of 'em done stole their horses 'n guns 'n boots. Now, you seen 'em or not?"

Henry opened his eyes.

"I have seen the two men you seek. They passed this way two hours ago by your white man's clock."

"Now, that's more like it. Which way'd they go?"

Henry looked disdainfully at the man, and then glanced up the hill.

"They did not go the way you have just come." He waved his hands. "And, the hills on the sides are too steep. There is only one way they could go." He pointed up the not-so-gentle slope. "The black white man had to stop many times to help the other up the hill. It was funny to watch them."

"Here that boys? They headin' toward the Cherokee capital. We get 'em for sure. That black bastard's back's gonna feel my lash 'fore we takes him back to Texas."

"I don't give a shit 'bout that," one of the men said. "All I want's my share of the bounty on that colored. You kin do whatever the hell you want with 'im, long's I git my money."

"Oh, you'll git your money, 'n a little fun besides."

He remounted, and looked down at Henry. "Thanks, big chief, you been a big help."

Henry, who had already gone back into his cross-legged, arm-folded pose and closed his eyes, didn't respond.

"Dang, that damn Injun is fast. He's already gone back to that there spirit world of his."

"Damn heathens got the strangest beliefs. Well, no matter. Let's ride boys. We're gonna git that bastard today."

With a clatter, and in a cloud of dust, the four men urged their horses up the hill, riding dangerously fast, Henry, who watched them through half-closed eyes, thought.

"Crazy white man," he muttered. "Do anything for

money."

He waited another hour to make sure the four men were well away before removing the cover over the cave entrance.

"You can come out now," he said. "The men chasing you are now chasing shadows."

13.

The three men, one black, one white, and one Indian, sat around a campfire eating one of two rabbits Henry had snared before their arrival. He supplemented the meat with some wild grasses he'd harvested and roasted in oak leaves in the hot ashes of the fire. Cratchett made a pot of his coffee.

"That was sho nuff some act you put on fer them fellas," Bass said. "I was peekin' at ya through them leaves, 'n when you looked up and ast that fella 'who disturb my spirit walk,' I plumb near bust out laughin' at the look on his face."

"Bass is right, Mr. Lone Tree," Cratchett said. "You are a natural actor. I've seen some famous people on stage, and you rival the best."

"You can call me Henry," Henry said. "Fooling people is easy. Most people see what they expect to see, so if you give them that, they ask no questions. Those men, like many whites, think of the Indian as superstitious and uncivilized. So, when I tell them I am on a spirit walk, they do not question. When I act strange, because they expect me to act strange, it does not surprise them."

"It sho is a better way of settlin' things than shootin', that's fo sho," Bass said. "It's jest too bad both sides in this danged war don' know 'bout yo way of settlin' things."

"Ah, the white man. He is good at fooling himself. Both sides have convinced themselves that they are right."

"Well, fo myself, I think the Union's right. They fightin' to free the slaves."

Henry's brow furrowed.

"Some of them are. But, most of them do not care that your people are in chains. They only want to keep the Union together, so they can steal more Indian land."

"I reckon you have some pretty strong feelings about the government in Washington, then," Cratchett said.

"Yes, I do. My father, and my father's father signed treaties with the white men from Washington, and got lots of promises. All those promises were broken as soon as some fool found gold, or some white settlers wanted more land to plow up. But, do not get me wrong. I have no sympathy for the southerners, the Confederates they call themselves. Already they've tried taking over this territory. They are no different than those in Washington as far as I am concerned."

"That must be difficult, not taking either side. I understand that the Cherokee are pretty much split over which side to support."

"Yes, it is as you say, difficult. Most of the full-blood Cherokee support the Union, while the half-breeds support the South. I am full-blood, but I do not think this should be the Indian's war. That is why I was out here alone. I had to get away from the constant bickering over which side to support. It looks like we Cherokee will make the same mistakes the whites did, and end up fighting cousin against cousin."

"I tell you one thing," Bass said. "They might be singin' 'n whoopin' 'n hollerin' when they goes off to war, but when the first shot's fired in the first battle, they all wants to run home to mama. I done seen men torn apart by cannon fire a layin' there with they guts spread all over the ground, cryin' for they mama."

Henry nodded. "The old men know this already," he said. "This is why they always send the young braves off to war. The young are too ignorant to know better."

"They lucky if they gits old," Bass said.

"So, Bass Reeves, what do you intend to do?"

"I gon' stay free, fo one thing. I was thinkin' mebbe I could go to Canada. I hears they accept black folk up there, 'n don' make 'em come back, like some folks in the North do."

"Canada is many suns journey from here."

"I don' care how long it take me to git there, long's I free at the other end."

Henry regarded him for a long time, rubbing at his cleft chin. "Have you ever been in Kansas or Missouri?"

"Fo I come here to Injun Territory, the only places I ever been was Arkansas and Texas . . . oh, and one time I went with ole man Reeves down ta Louisiana, but we was only there fo a few hours."

"So, you plan to travel through territory you do not know, to a place you have never been? You will not last seven suns doing it like that."

"What you recommendin' I do, then?" Bass's face was a study in frustration. "Everybody tellin' me what I can't do all the time. I need somebody to tell me what I *can* do fo a change."

"There is one thing you can do, but before you decide, you must think on it for a while."

"Humph, all's I been doin' is thinkin'. I been thinkin' 'bout bein' free. So, I reckon iffen you tell me what you got in mind, I can think on it a bit."

"You could stay here, here in the Cherokee Nation," Henry said.

"What? You 'spect me to stay here with a buncha Injuns what got slaves, and what done sided with the rebels?"

Henry held an open hand up.

"Before you go off half-cocked, Bass Reeves, hear me out. Not all Cherokee sided with the South. Sure, when the soldiers from Washington left and the Confederates came, we signed treaties with them. We Indians have been doing that since the first white man came to this land. But, only some of the tribes, and some of the men in the tribes, actually threw their lot in with the southerners. The full-blood Cherokee like me, follow John Ross, and when he saw what the southerners were up to, he refused to let his warriors join them. Only the half-breeds follow that fool, Stand Watie."

"Who in blazes is John Ross and Stand Watie? Am I s'pose to know 'em?"

"No, Bass Reeves, I do not expect you to know them, but I will tell you who they are. John Ross is a half-breed, part Scot, part Cherokee, but his heart is all Cherokee. He is the main chief of the Cherokee. He is the one who signed the treaty with the southern colonel. But, he is also the one who told the Cherokee not to fight the soldiers from Washington. Stand Watie is also a half-breed, but his heart has always been more white than Indian. He raised a regiment to fight for the rebels. They made him a colonel, and that fat fool thinks it is because they respect him."

"Okay, so I need to avoid this Watie fella. How am I gon' know 'im iffen I see 'im?"

"You will need someone to guide you who knows the territory." Henry looked at Cratchett. "I do not mean to insult you, Preacher Cratchett, but you know nothing about Cherokee land."

"No insult taken, Henry. You are, of course, absolutely right. This is my first time in the Cherokee Nation."

"So, where I gon' find this guide?"

Henry thumped his chest with his right fist.

"Here, Bass Reeves. I, Henry Lone Tree, will be your guide."

Bass's eyes went wide and his mouth gaped open. Seldom in his life had he been surprised. And now, in a short span of time, he'd been hit by two surprises that slammed into him like a sack of wet cotton. First, a white man who treated him as an equal, and put his life in jeopardy on his behalf. And now, an Indian, a member of a slaveholding tribe, was offering to help him keep his freedom. The world was surely a more complicated place than he'd ever suspected. But, he wasn't quite ready to grab this bait like a hungry fish.

"Why you do that fo me? You don' even know me."

"It is true that I just met you. But, the spirit tells me that you are a good man, a special man, and that it is my duty to guide and protect you. I dreamed of a big man, dark like a bear, with the eyes of an eagle, and the heart of a mountain lion, who would come to me for help. You, Bass Reeves, are the man in my dreams."

While Bass wasn't particularly superstitious, he'd seen many things that couldn't be explained, and he did believe in the power of dreams. If this Henry Lone Tree dreamed that he was to be his guide, well, so be it.

"Okay, you my guide. Where we gon' go from here?"

"For now, we go nowhere. The slave hunters will be sent off chasing rabbits by any other Cherokee they meet, and will not come back this way. My spirit totem has told me that this place is safe. While we wait, I will begin to teach you what you need to know to be a free man here in Cherokee Nation."

Cratchett stood and dusted off his trousers.

"Well, looks to be my mission is complete, Bass," he said. "I promised to get you to safety, and I reckon staying with Henry here is the safest thing you can do right now, so I'd best be on my way. Got a lot of other souls to save."

"Don' rush off, Preacher man," Bass said. "Least ways, stay 'n have some supper. T'morrow's time enough fo you to get on with yo soul-savin.'"

Cratchett sniffed the air. "I am feeling a mite puckish. A meal before I set out on my sojourn would not be amiss. Very well, I will wait until morning to take my leave."

14.

Cratchett ended up staying five more days. He couldn't resist butting in as Henry began the education of Bass to the ways of Indian Territory.

On the first day, they sat near the fire Henry was using to cook two rabbits he'd snared.

"The first thing you must learn," he said to Bass. "Is how to make your way around the land."

"Oh, he already knows that," Cratchett said. "Bass's got eyes as sharp as a hawk. Why, he spotted them slave catchers' tracks in a mess of tracks that made no sense to me at all."

Henry looked quizzically at Bass. "Is this true? Do you know how to read trail signs?"

"Uh, yeah. That's cuz I pays attention, 'n I remembers good."

"That is good." Henry nodded. "Do you know the animal signs?"

"Well, I knows horses and cows, 'n I reckon I know the difference 'twixt a elk and a mountain lion."

"But, can you tell if an elk has been injured, or if a mountain lion is starving?"

"Naw, how you gon' tell that from tracks?"

"Hah. There are ways, and I will teach you. You have much to learn."

"Well, I guess you best git to learnin' me, then."

"I will, in good time. It will not come in one sun. There is, though, one other thing that is very important for you to learn. You must learn to ride small in the saddle."

"Huh?" Bass and Cratchett said in unison.

Henry chuckled. "You are a big man, and you are a black man. The slave catchers were looking for a big black man riding a horse. If you do not want people to know who you are, you must learn to be smaller when you ride."

"How I gon' do that?"

"Do not worry, my friend. I will teach you."

That was the first lesson he taught Bass.

It wasn't as simple as he made it sound, especially for someone as big as Bass. Used by Indian warriors to make themselves smaller targets in battle, it involved hunching the shoulders and hunkering down over a horse's neck. It was so unnatural, Bass reflexively rebelled, but Henry was as stubborn as a mule, and kept making him do it over and over again until he was satisfied.

Finally, by the end of the second day, he pronounced Bass as ready to ride small in the saddle as he was ever going to be.

All the while he was teaching him riding, identifying various animals by their tracks and droppings, and how to read the weather, he began teaching him the basics of the Cherokee language, and even a few of the hand signs the Plains tribes used among themselves and with the trappers and traders who visited them before they were forced off their land.

And, all the while, Cratchett stood behind Henry, critiquing everything he did, pointing out where thought he was teaching Bass all the wrong things, and bemoaning the lack of religion in his instruction. That latter complaint caused Henry to whirl on him with a snarl on his face.

"You white men think you are the only ones with your so-called religion. Always coming to Indian lands to convert the heathens. *You* are the heathens, the way you put other people in chains, destroy the land, and mistreat the animals." His ruddy complexion darkened and his eyes blazed. "We Indians believe in the Great Spirit, and the spirits that are in all things, the animals, the trees, and the lands. Yes, we sometimes make war on each other, but not for land or power, but in self-defense, or to avenge a great wrong, and often, rather than killing our enemy, it is enough to get close enough to touch him. We call that counting *coup*. Sure, many moons ago, the Cherokee and the Creek fought great battles, but today, we leave as neighbors."

Cratchett backed up, holding his hands up in surrender.

"Whoa, Henry, I didn't mean any disrespect. I was just concerned that Bass's spiritual development not be neglected."

Henry let out a great puff of air. "I will teach him to respect all living things, but the most important thing I will teach him is to have respect for himself."

"You ain't got to worry, Preacher Cratchett," Bass said. "I believes in God, 'n even though I can't read the Bible, I done 'membered ever thing you done told me. I think Henry's right, though, if we really gon' be Christian, we got to respect all life, not jest the ones what got the same color skin we got."

Cratchett smiled. "Well, I'll be dog, I do believe you're right. I see what you mean. You know, I think I can work that thought into my sermons."

"Hmph," Henry said. "Then, you had better go back to the land of the white man and preach, because they need it much more than we Indians do."

"I fear, my friend, that you are right. But, I think I would have to search hard to find a congregation that would listen."

"But, Preacher Cratchett, you done said lots of them Quakers 'n even some Baptists 'n others, b'lieve the same way you do. Mebbe you oughta find a settlement of folks like that 'n preach to them, 'n 'courage them to go out 'n preach to others."

Cratchett closed his eyes, cocked his head, and laid a finger on his temple. His eyes snapped open, and he snapped his finger. "By jingies, Bass, you might not know how to read or write, but you're smarter than most men I ever met. You just hit on what my mission has to be. I need to go back home and teach missionaries to go out and save my own people."

"When are you leaving?" Henry asked with a sarcastic tone.

Cratchett chuckled. "Soon, my friend, soon. And then, you can have your student all to yourself."

It's not that I don't like you, preacher. It's just that only one set of hands can fire a bow, and you, being a natural-born teacher, cannot help yourself. You interfere, not from bad thoughts, but because it is just in you to teach. Bass has a teacher—me. You need to go and find your proper students."

"I know, Henry, and I do know I can be quite intrusive at times. But, you are absolutely right. I will leave come sunup, and just in case I should leave before the two of you wake up, know that I will pray for you each night."

"Thank you, Preacher Cratchett," Bass said. "That's much appreciated."

"Yes," Henry said. "Until this war is over, we will need all the praying we can get."

The next morning at sunup, when Bass and Henry woke up, the preacher, the roan, and the preacher's bag, was gone.

Henry showed Bass the roan's tracks, heading east.

"You know," he said. "I will miss him, even though I would never tell him that."

"Yeah, I gon' miss 'im, too," Bass said. "But, I ain't gon' never forget what he done taught me."

The Marshal and The Madam

1..

"Howdy, Miz Belle. How you doin' today?" He tipped his hat as he walked toward the porch.

"I'm doing just fine. How are you, Bass?" the woman replied, smiling.

While she wasn't entirely unpleasant to look at, with her square jaw and eyes set a little too close together, she was not what one would call a great beauty, nothing like the painted ladies who worked in the saloons, dance halls and brothels throughout the Indian Territory. Despite the lack of classic beauty, though, whenever she rode into town, or walked into a room, people took notice. It might have been her sense of style. When she went riding side saddle, she always wore a dark velvet riding habit, and a man's hat with plumes, and around her waist she carried two revolvers. The fact that she was an expert rider and a crack shot was known by all, and also impressed them. She cut an impressive figure wherever she went. She didn't encourage people to believe the things they did, but she didn't discourage them either.

The same things could be said of the man, Bass Reeves. He stood six feet, two inches tall, and his two-hundred-pound frame was well muscled and broad shouldered, with hands at the ends of his arms that were big enough to crush a man's head. He, too, was a snappy dresser, and wore two Colt .45 caliber revolvers, butt first around his waist, and was such a good shot with either hand that in his home in Arkansas, he was often barred from entering shooting competitions. He was also a man who took pride in his appearance, usually wearing a nicely turned out jacket of gray, brown, or black, and a Stetson with a straight brim. His boots, unless he was in disguise, were always polished to a high gloss. When he walked into a room, everyone, man or woman, stopped what he or she was doing and gawked. Unlike Belle, though, he could, when he chose, become almost invisible. During his time in Indian Territory during the war, his Indian friends had taught him to ride 'small in the saddle.' Not only did this make for a smaller target for ambushers to shoot at, it helped to disguise his large frame from a distance, enabling him at times to ride right up to fugitives unnoticed until it was too late.

A person could search Indian Territory for a lifetime and not find two more unlikely friends. She was short, he was tall, much taller than the average man. She was petite, and he was large and muscular. Her skin, when she stayed out of the sun, was the color of ivory, and she had long, brown hair, while his skin was the color of polished mahogany, and his hair was short, curly, and beginning to grow gray at the temples. She had come from a family that, though they themselves had owned no slaves, had been friends with many who did, and had supported the southern slaveholders in the North-South war. He had been born a slave, had run away to Indian Territory during the war after a dispute with his master, returning to his home in Arkansas in 1863, after President Lincoln issued the proclamation freeing the slaves in the rebelling states. Despite these differences, they found pleasure in each other's company.

"I'm fair to middlin', Miz Belle," he said.

"It's been a while. Where you off to this time?"

"I got me some warrants to serve over to Fort Sill."

"Well, I'm pleased you took the time to drop in and visit a spell," she said. "Would you like a cup of coffee, or maybe some fresh-made lemonade?"

"Why, coffee would do just fine."

Belle Starr, born Myra Maybelle Shirley, in Carthage, Missouri, reached for the silver coffee urn on the carved wooden table at her side. She poured the brown brew into a fancy porcelain cup, and handed it up to the man who now stood at the empty chair on the other side of the table. He took a sip of the hot liquid, and then sat.

The two sat in silence for a long time. Finally, the silence was broken when a man of middle height, his dark brown hair flowing back and down over his head in waves, displaying a high, broad forehead, and piercing brown eyes. A neat mustache and goatee gave him a sinister appearance, until he smiled. It had been his smile that had attracted Belle to him in the first place.

Sam Starr was the son of Tom Starr, part Irish, part Cherokee, who had for a long time been leader of the Starr gang, a band of pro-treaty Cherokee who, after being attacked by those who opposed the treaties with the U.S. Government, had avenged the attacks with a reign of terror. Sam had assumed the leadership after his father got too old to keep pace, and had added cattle theft to the long list of crimes the gang was involved in. He had, though, confined his crimes to actions against Indian residents of the territory, as far as people knew, which kept the U.S. marshals off his tail.

"Well, hello, deputy. Ain't seen you in a while," the man said.

"Howdy to you too, Sam. What you been up to lately?"

Sam's smile broadened, and he looked down at the woman. "Ain't been up to nothin' a'tall. Ain't that right, Belle?"

They shared a look and a smile. "No, Bass, he hasn't been up to anything."

Sam Starr poured himself a cup of coffee, and took a sip.

"What about you, deputy," he said. "What you been up to lately?"

"Same as always," Bass said. "Got me some fugitives here in the territory that I got to take back to Fort Smith."

"More poor fools for Judge Parker to hang, eh?" Starr laughed.

Bass didn't. He frowned. "Ain't like that. Folks call Judge Parker the Hangin' Judge, but that's 'cause so many of the people what come into his court done things that call for hangin'. Fact is, though, he ain't sent all that many people to the gallows."

"Whatever you say, deputy. Say, Belle, I gotta ride over to Porum Gap to the general store to pick up some supplies. Nice talking to ya, deputy." He touched a finger to the brim of his hat, stepped off the porch and headed for the corral attached to the large barn off to the side of the ranch house.

After he'd ridden away to the north, Bass finished his coffee and stood. "Well, Miz Belle, I got to be movin' myself. My guard and cook's waitin' for me up at Porum Gap. We got a long ride ahead of us."

Belle stood. "You sure you can't stay a mite longer, Bass. I was going to play the piano a little later."

"Well now, you know ain't nothin' I like more 'n listenin' to you play, but I really best be movin' on. Maybe on the way back to Fort Smith, we can stop and listen to you play."

"I'll hold you to that, Bass Reeves."

Bass mounted his grey stallion, tipped his hat, and rode away. When he was out of sight, the front door opened, and two men walked out onto the porch.

"You know, Belle, I just don't understand why you so friendly with that colored lawman, or any colored man, for that matter," the older of the two said.

"You wouldn't understand, Frank," she said. "You, Jesse, and Cole and his brothers still fighting the war. It's over, and the colored been freed. We have to accept that."

The younger of the two men ran a hand through his slicked back brown hair. "I got nothin' agin colored, but ain't no lawman ever done favors for the James family, 'n I know Cole feels the same on the part of the Younger clan. The Yankees might've won the war, but it ain't hardly over long's we got southern warriors willin' to take up the gun. We can make sure the Yankees and all their sympathizers pay for what they done to our homes."

The trio, to a casual observer, seemed a most unlikely matchup. Belle Starr, born to John Shirley and Eliza Hatfield Shirley, had been brought up in relative affluence in Carthage, where her father, after giving up farming, had owned an inn, a livery, and a blacksmith shop, located in Carthage's town square. A pillar of the town community, he'd been one of the cofounders of a school for young women there, where young Myra Maybelle, who in her teens took to calling herself Belle, received a classical education. She had known the James and Younger families, local farmers, from childhood, and like them, her family had supported the southern side in the fratricidal War of Secession. When Carthage was sacked by Union forces, Belle's family had moved south to Texas, while the James and Younger boys had joined the Bushwhackers, Confederate sympathizers in Missouri and Kansas, such as William Quantrill, who raided, robbed, and killed, and spread terror throughout the war, and after it ended, had turned to lives of crime. When pressure from the law built up in Kansas and

Missouri, they would often flee to Indian Territory, and because of the family connections, sought safe haven at the ranch Belle shared with her second husband, Sam Starr, leader of the notorious Starr clan, a group of Cherokee bandits who stole cattle, and committed various other crimes in the territory. Starr's father, Tom Starr, half-Cherokee, half-Irish, was known as one of the most vicious criminals in the territory, and before his death was reported to have killed over a hundred men. Although she knew that providing shelter for wanted men was a crime, she was from a culture that valued family and friends over government, and in addition to having grown up with the James and Younger families, as a young woman she'd been romantically involved with Cole Younger, a relationship that ended when her family moved to Texas.

The relationship, though, still occupied a place in her mind, for the area on the Canadian River where she and Sam had built their ranch had been named Younger's Bend, many believed in honor of Cole Younger.

Sam Starr had, up to that time, not been accused of committing a crime that fell under the jurisdiction of Judge Isaac Parker's court in Fort Smith, Arkansas, so, even though Bass had heard the rumors about him, since he had no warrant for his arrest, he did nothing. The other reason was his admiration for Belle. Her polish and education, and the friendly, even-handed treatment she accorded him was the cause—that, and her piano playing. She did not act intimidated by his size, nor did she seem to act friendly to him just because he was a lawman; in fact, she seemed to like him despite that fact. She just accepted him for what he was. For his part, he chose to ignore the gossipers who labeled her 'the Bandit Queen,' believing instead that this was just idle gossip due to her association with the likes of Sam Starr.

The respect was mutual.

"Just don't be bringing your war to my home, Jesse James," she said. "And, I see that look in your eyes when you talk about Bass. You steer clear of him, you hear?"

James held his hands up in surrender. "I ain't got no quarrel with him. Long's he leaves me alone, I'll leave him alone."

"Don't you be getting up to any of your ruffian ways down here. If you do, and they issue a warrant for you out of Fort Smith, Bass *will* come after you, and word is, he always gets his man."

"Let's hope it don't come to that," Frank James said. "I know he's a friend of yours, and I'd plumb hate to have to kill him."

"And," she said. "I'd hate for him to kill you."

"You think that boy would stand a chance against me? Hell fire, Belle, I done killed more men than I can count on all my fingers 'n toes. What do you think I'd do to that boy if he was to come after me?"

She faced him down. "If you were smart, you'd give yourself up. You see those two sidearms he wears around his waist? Well, he's a dead shot with either of them, in either hand, and he can hit a hickory nut at the top of a tree from a hundred yards. He's such a good marksman, over in Arkansas they won't let him enter the shooting competitions."

He shrugged. "Okay, so I wouldn't challenge him to a draw down. There's more 'n one way to take care of a meddlesome lawman."

"Now, you listen here, Frank James, I don't want to hear nothing about you bushwhacking, Bass Reeves, you got that?"

"Aw, come on, Belle, I ain't said nothin' 'bout bushwhackin' him."

"You think I was born yesterday. I know what you meant, and I will hear none of that if you want to be welcome in my house."

"Okay, Belle, me 'n Jesse won't be goin' after your pet lawman. That make you happy?"

"What would make me happy is if you and your brother would stay out of sight. I don't want the neighbors gossiping about the notorious James boys living at Younger's Bend."

What she really wanted to say was that she would be happier if they packed their gear and took themselves back to Missouri or Kansas, and left her in peace. Instead, she slapped her riding crop against her leg and strode off the porch.

"I'm going for a ride to clear my head," she said. "You boys try not to cause any trouble while I'm gone."

Jesse, though younger, was the principal initiator of most of their escapades, took his hat off and bowed deeply in her direction.

"Your wish is our command, Miz Belle," he said, a mocking expression on his youthful face. "Me 'n Frank will be as quiet as field mice."

Belle rolled her eyes, but couldn't hold back a smile. As bloodthirsty and violent as he could be, Jesse James had a magnetic personality, and like most people, she was not immune to his charm.

2.

After nearly three weeks in the area around Fort Sill, in west-central Oklahoma Territory, and with just a few days left on his thirty-day limit, Bass didn't stop at Younger's Bend on his way back to Fort Smith with a wagon-load of fugitives. After such long absences, he was always anxious to get home to his farm near Van Buren, and spend some time with his wife and children.

After getting his posse man to fill out the paperwork he was required to submit, which he signed by making an X at the bottom, and paying his friend Henry Lone Tree his scout fee for the month, he turned the prisoners over to the jailer and made his way to Marshal James Fagan's office in the Fort Smith Federal Courthouse.

"Howdy, Bass," Fagan said. "Have a seat. How was your trip?" Fagan looked up from some papers he'd been studying and waved Bass to the chair beside his desk. He toyed with his beard as he eyed the black deputy. "I hear you stopped at Younger's Bend on your way out."

That Fagan knew of his movements, even over a hundred miles away from Fort Smith, didn't surprise Bass. Gossip in the territory spread like a wild fire on a dry prairie.

Bass's relationship with Belle Starr had long been an issue between the two men. Fagan was among those who were convinced that Belle was heavily involved in illegal activities, and he worried that Bass, despite his reputation for enforcing the law without fear or favor, would not be able to carry out his duties when, as he knew it inevitably would, the time came to serve a warrant on the woman.

"Yes, sir. I stopped and had coffee with Miz Belle."

"You know, Bass, I'm not one to tell you who you can associate with, but I worry sometimes about your relationship with the Starr clan."

Bass sat forward in his chair.

"I know, marshal," he said. "I done heard all the stories, 'n I'm pretty sure the ones I hear 'bout Sam Starr are mostly true. After all, he's the son of Tom Starr, one of the meanest Cherokee that ever lived. But, his crimes are against Injuns, and that's a matter for the tribal police. And, I also done heard all the stories 'bout Miz Belle, too. But, ain't a one of 'em ever been proved. They's just rumors. You don't issue warrants based on rumors, do you?"

Fagan tugged at his beard, his broad brow furrowed. "Well, of course not, Bass. But, with so much smoke, there's bound to be a little fire somewhere."

"Well, if I see any fire, I'll sho nuff try to put it out."

"What does that mean?"

"It means, if somebody show me some proof that Miz Belle done broke the law, and Judge Parker issues a warrant, I'll go and bring her in."

Fagan stared across the desk. Bass's face was as immobile as the trunk of an oak tree. Fingering the silver marshal's badge he wore on his vest, he nodded. "Danged if I don't believe you would. Well, let's hope it don't come to that. Now, I know you want to get on home and spend some time with Nellie and them kids of yours, but I got another stack of warrants, so I'm gonna need you back here in a week."

Bass stood, his serious expression easing. "Sure nuff, marshal. I'll be here soon's I get some new fence put up in my south pasture. Prob'ly won't be more 'n four, five days."

Fagan smiled at his broad back as he left. Maybe he need not worry about his best deputy after all.

3.

At the very moment that Bass was riding out of Fort Smith, heading toward his farm near Van Buren, Belle Starr stood on the porch of her ranch house at Younger's Bend, in Indian Territory, watching three horsemen approaching down the road leading to the main gate to the property. She recognized the roans ridden by Frank and Jesse James, and when they were close enough that she recognized the third rider, she frowned.

The last person she wanted to see was Cole Younger. Her husband, Sam, knew of her relationship with Cole when they both were teens, and, with the temper he'd inherited from his father, Tom, she worried about his reaction to Cole being in Oklahoma, and worse, in their home.

She tried not to let her worry show as the three men stopped their horses and dismounted, or to show the tingle of excitement as Cole stepped up close to her, too close for comfort. Their relationship had never gone beyond her looking at him with stars in her eyes, but she had to admit that he'd only gotten more handsome as he'd gotten older. If Sam ever saw her looking at Cole with her eyes bugged and her mouth half open like she knew it was, he'd go crazy, and there would be bloodshed. Despite the ties of friendship that existed between her and these men and their families, she would have to find a way to encourage them to make their stays at Younger's Bend short.

"Hi, Belle," Younger said.

She swallowed hard. "Hello, Cole. What are you doing here?"

She didn't need to ask the question, because she already knew the answer; it was the same as it was for all of her former friends from Missouri. He was on the run from the law. Like the James brothers, Cole Younger and his brothers and cousins had been Bushwhackers during the war, laying waste to settlements that supported the Union, killing Union soldiers and sympathizers alike, stealing Union supplies, and when the war ended, instead of laying down their arms and returning to farming, had continued to ply the trade they'd learned in the war, by robbing banks and stage coaches, and killing anyone who got in their way. Letting them stay here at Younger's Bend was, she knew, a big mistake, one that could get everyone into trouble, especially in light of her husband, Sam's, sideline. But bonds of kinship were important. She'd been taught never to turn away a friend in need.

And, when that friend was as handsome as Cole Younger, it was impossible to say no to a request for help.

He looked down at her, his trademark smile causing her knees to tremble.

"Just thought I'd come down and see how you were doin', Belle," he said. "I been meanin' to come down and visit ever since I heard your first husband, Jim Reed, got himself kilt. Hear you done married yourself a redskin? What's his Injun name?"

Her cheeks flamed red.

"There's no need to use words like that, Cole. I don't allow it in my house. Sam's part Cherokee, part Irish. He doesn't have an Indian name, so you can call him Sam, or maybe it'd be better if you just called him Mister Starr."

Younger laughed derisively.

"No offense meant, Belle. You think *Mister* Star would mind if I hung out here for a few days?"

Of course, he'll mind, she thought, but he wouldn't say anything. Even though he was as deadly as his father had been, he was completely smitten by her, and would do anything she asked of him. Besides, Sam also understood the obligations of family and clan as well, if not better, than Belle did. He wouldn't object to their presence unless one of them crossed the line that defined his honor.

"No, he won't mind," she said. "But, you'll have to stay in the bunkhouse with the hands."

He looked disappointed, but smiled at her. "That won't be a problem, Belle, no problem at all."

"And, Cole," she said. "I'll tell you the same thing I've told Frank and Jesse; while you're here, I don't want any trouble."

He bowed, a mocking smile on his face. "I give you my word, Belle. I will not start any trouble."

4.

Bass's homecoming was a raucous one. With ten children ranging in age from six to seventeen, the place was always noisy, but never more so than when he returned from one of his long trips into Indian Territory.

Before leaving Fort Smith, he'd stopped at a general store and bought gifts for Nellie and each of the children, gifts that were greeted with cheers and hugs.

That first day back home, he spent time listening to each child tell him what he or she had done while he was gone, paying particular attention to the older ones' recitation of the tasks he'd set them around the ranch, and happy to see that each had completed everything assigned. When the last child was finally tucked in and pretending to be asleep, he and Nellie retired to the front porch, where they sat in silence, enjoying the solitude and companionship.

From the second day, and for five days thereafter, he was busy stringing fence, replacing broken boards in the barn, and putting in pipes to enable Nellie to pump water into the kitchen, something he'd seen in one of the big houses near Fort Smith. One day, he thought, maybe someone would even figure out a way to put a toilet inside the house, so they wouldn't have to make the long trek to the outhouse on cold winter nights.

On the sixth day, the compulsion to get back on the trail of wanted fugitives was just too strong. At mid-morning, he called Nellie out to the porch.

"You leavin' already?" she asked, even though she knew the answer. This was always how he prepared to leave on one of his trips into the territory.

He put his large hands on her shoulder and pulled her close. "Yeah, hon. Marshal Kagan's got a whole buncha warrants for me."

She put her arms around his waist and hugged hard.

"Bass, I wish you didn't have to do this. I worry 'bout you so much when you go out there."

"There's no need to worry," he said. "I know how to take care of myself."

She pulled back and looked up into his eyes. "I know, but I still worry. You hurry up and get on back here, you hear me? Me 'n the children miss you so much when you gone."

"I will, baby girl, 'cause I miss y'all, too."

He kissed her on the forehead, patted her shoulder, and left her standing there on the porch as he walked to the stable to saddle his horse.

She was still standing there, when he rode out of the stable. He slowed as he passed the front of the house, tipped his hat to her, and then, kicked his horse's flanks, urging the animal into a gentle trot.

It was approaching mid-day when he arrived in Fort Smith and presented himself in Fagan's office.

Fagan gave him a wry look. "You're back a few days early, Bass," he said. "But, I'm not really surprised. How'd your wife take it this time?"

"She ain't none too happy, but she knows that it's the money from this job that lets us live nice lives. She's a tough woman, but I think she gets put out havin' to keep track of all them young'uns by herself."

"Can't say's I blame her. How many you got now?'

Bass had to think a few seconds. "Ten, last count," he said. "I 'spect they can be a hand full, for sure. But, the oldest ones help with the little ones, so it can't be too bad. I think she just misses me. Now, marshal, what you got for me?"

Fagan shuffled some papers on his desk.

"Got a bank robber, a couple of land swindlers, and a fella who killed his friend in an argument over a card game. You ought to be able to get all these done in a couple of weeks."

They went through the usual routine; Fagan held up each warrant so that Bass could see and memorize it, while he read the particulars of each fugitive. Even after several years of Bass's performance, he was still amazed at his ability to retain such a volume of information. But, retain it, he did. He had, thus far, never made a mistake, even when he had as many as ten or fifteen warrants. Once, Bass had brought in sixteen wanted men, men he'd located and arrested in less than twenty days in settlements and hideouts throughout Indian Territory. And, unlike many of the deputies, Bass didn't often get into shootouts with the men he pursued, instead, often tricking them into surrendering. On the few occasions when a wanted man had been foolish enough to engage in gunplay, Bass had arranged for a suitable funeral, after getting witnesses to write a report of the incident for him, to which he affixed his 'X' dutifully.

Satisfied that Bass had memorized the content of the four warrants, Fagan stacked them neatly and passed them across the desk. Bass went through them once more, peering intently at each, and then folded them neatly and tucked them in his jacket pocket. He would later, upon encountering a wanted man, remove them, select the correct one without fail, and let the man see it to verify that he was being placed under arrest. Sometimes, the man would already be in handcuffs when this occurred.

Bass stood, saluted the marshal, and left. Outside the courthouse, he met up with his cook, a freckle-faced red head named Patrick Donovan, the driver of his prisoner wagon, Robert Jefferson, a tall, skinny man with unruly brown hair, who wore a battered derby hat, and carried a shotgun rather than a revolver. He would meet up with his posse man, his friend, Henry Lone Tree, west of the deadline, a north-south line about eighty miles west of Fort Smith, beyond which a lawman traveled at his own peril. Outlaws in Indian Territory often posted notices near the deadline, warning the deputy marshals, sometimes by name, that if they crossed the line, they would be killed, and during time since Bass became a deputy, several deputies *had* been killed in the territory. Bass had been the personal subject of several such notices, messages that his guard wagon driver or cook had read to him. Each time, he'd taken the notice, folded it neatly, and tucked it into his pocket. He'd been shot at several times, once a bullet had even punched through the crown of his hat, missing his skull by a hair's breadth, and one outlaw had shot off his saddle horn, but he'd not been injured.

In one incident, he'd cornered two outlaws, and they'd gotten the drop on him. He'd asked them if, before they shot him, they would read a letter he'd received from his wife. He took a folded paper from his pocket, and when one of the men had reached for it, Bass had grabbed his gun hand. He'd pulled his own revolver and smashed the other man over the head with it, before subduing the man he'd grabbed.

His exploits were known throughout the territory, and had earned him the nickname, 'The Indomitable Marshal.' His knowledge of the tribal customs and languages had earned him the respect of most of the Indian inhabitants, and his tracking ability, dogged persistence, strength, and bravery, caused the territory's outlaws to hate and fear him in equal measure.

His first stop after the deadline was at Henry Lone Tree's farm. Henry often served as his scout and posse man. When the two of them worked together, fugitives had no chance of remaining hidden. The two of them together brought dread to all evil doers.

5.

Henry had been awaiting Bass's arrival. He knew that his friend wouldn't remain absent from the territory for too long.

A member of the Choctaw tribe, Henry had been the first friendly face Bass encountered when he'd run away from Texas to the territory during the war. Bass had been given by his original owner, William Reeves, to his older son, George. When the war started, George Reeves was made a colonel in the Confederate forces, and took Bass along as his orderly. One night, while his master slept, Bass slipped away and headed north to Indian Territory. He'd crossed the Red River, and was in unfamiliar territory when, unknown to him, a band of slave hunters had begun tracking him. Henry Lone Tree, out hunting, had seen the lone black man making his way through the bush, and noticed the gang of white men close behind him. Reading the situation correctly, Henry had intercepted Bass, informed him of the danger closing in, and helped him elude his would-be captors. From that moment, the two had become friends.

When the familiar grey stallion came into view down the road, followed by two wagons, Henry stood, his hand shading his eyes against the glare of the morning sun, and watched them approach.

The two wagons stopped at the gate, fifty yards from his front porch, but Bass kept riding until he was only a few feet away.

"Hello, Bass," he said. "How many evil men are we going after this time?"

"Howdy to you too, Henry," Bass said. "I'm doin' fine, how 'bout you?"

Henry laughed. "You have been back in the land of the white men too long, my friend. You can see that I am alive and well, as I can see that you are as well."

Bass frowned. He threw his leg over and dismounted. "You're right, Henry. Guess I done learned the old ways again. I sure can see you doin' good. We got us five fugitives to catch this time. Couple of 'em s'posed to be over by Shawnee, 'n the rest I hear might be 'round Chickasha. I reckon we be able to pick 'em up in 'bout a week, ten days at most."

Henry held up his left hand and counted the fingers of his right. "Hm, that comes to just thirty dollars tops. Hardly worth leaving the farm for that."

"Yeah," Bass said. "But, where else you gon' get paid that much for doin' next to nothin'?"

"You think this will be that easy?"

"Yeah. 'Cept for the robber and the fella who killed his friend over a card game, they ain't really likely to be dangerous. I don't even think them two will put up any kinda fight. Won't be no harder than the time you 'n me was on the run from them slave catchers."

"Well, since you put it like that, let me get my rifle and we can get going."

6.

"Well, Belle, I reckon we done overstayed our welcome, haven't we?" Cole Younger stood on the porch, his hands shoved into the pockets of his brown nankeen trousers, his head cocked to the side.

Belle, wearing her dark, blue riding habit, a derby with a peacock feather stuck in the band, and a riding crop in her right hand, frowned as she faced him.

"It's not that I'm not happy to see you, Cole," she said. "But, because of Sam's father, and the fact that he's now head of the clan, the law over in Arkansas watches us with eagle eyes. If they ever found out I've been letting you and the James boys stay here, we'd both be in a peck of trouble. And, trouble is something we don't need right now."

"Way I hear it, it's not just old Tom Starr the law's interested in. I hear that man of yours gets himself mixed up in some pretty nasty goings on from time to time."

Belle's frown deepened and her cheeks turned red. Even though she was well aware that when Tom Starr became too old to keep pace with the clan's activities, Sam, as the oldest son, had inherited the leadership of the Starr clan, the biggest gang of thieves and ne'er-do-wells in Cherokee land, but she didn't like having it thrown in her face, least of all by someone to whom she'd extended the hospitality of her home, and someone who was so far on the wrong side of the law himself, he couldn't even see the line.

"He's been sticking to the territory," she said. "He's done nothing to draw attention from the law in Arkansas."

"Then, what you got to worry 'bout, girl?"

She stamped her foot on the uneven boards of the porch. "Look, Cole, I don't want to get into an argument with you about this. I just think it'd be better if you found another place to stay. Sam will be back by noon, he's bringing in some horses we're putting up for sale. It really might be best if you were gone when he gets here."

Smiling broadly, he nodded.

"Ah, now I see what the problem is. Your man's jealous of me. He know about me 'n you from when we were young?"

Her cheeks turned redder. "No, and don't you even think about telling him anything, you hear me, because you and I both know nothing ever happened between us?"

"Now, don't you be frettin' that pretty head of yours, Belle," he said. "What happened before is just between you 'n me. But, if he don't know about us, why is he so hot on me leaving?"

"It's not just you, Cole. He wants Frank and Jesse gone, too."

"What's he got against them?"

"I told you, we don't want trouble with the law. Our neighbors see you three hanging around, they talk. All it takes is for one of them to recognize one of you, and we've got more trouble than we need."

She had a painful look on her face, and was on the verge of tears.

"Okay, Belle, I get it. Don't you worry," he said. "I've got no desire to cause you any trouble. I'll go get Frank and Jesse, and we'll be on the road in less'n an hour."

She breathed deeply. "Thank you, Cole," she said. "I'm sorry to have to do this. We've been friends a long time, but there's just too much at stake. You understand?"

"Of course, I do, Belle. Maybe when things get better, I can come back and get to know you and that man of yours. Show him that I ain't such a bad man."

"Maybe," she said. But, there was no conviction in her voice. One thing she knew for sure, handsome as he might be, Cole Younger was in deed a *very* bad man.

7.

Bass and his crew found the bank robber holed up in a line shack just north of Shawnee.

The rundown structure, with boards missing from the walls, corrugated tin sheets rusted and turned up at the ends, and oil cloth covering the many broken windows, sat back from the rutted trail, against a low hill covered with ivy and blackberry bushes. A trail of white smoke curled up from the iron chimney pipe. For someone trying to hide from the law, he hadn't shown much skill. He'd left a trail, according to Henry, a blind man could have followed, and had picked a structure that offered no protection from rifle fire, and with only one door, effectively trapped him inside.

Bass and Henry smiled at each other as they halted their horses on the trail about a hundred feet from the shack.

"How are we going to do this?" Henry asked.

"I'm just gon' go up and ask him to give himself up," Bass replied.

"You sure he will do that?"

"Only one way to find out."

"You know, one of these days, you're gonna to do that, and someone's gonna shoot you."

"I reckon if he was gon' shoot, he'd of done it by now," Bass said. "We wasn't exactly quiet comin' up on this place, and we standing here in plain sight. Naw, I reckon he's just waitin' for me to give him the chance to give up."

Henry shrugged. "Okay, old friend. It's your funeral. I'll make sure you get a good burial."

Bass dismounted and walked up to the door of the shack. He rapped on the warped wood.

"Who's out there?" a voice called from inside the shack.

"You James Tucker?" Bass asked.

"Who want to know?"

"I'm Deputy U.S. Marshal Bass Reeves, 'n I come to arrest you. Come on out with your hands up."

Henry, the prisoner wagon driver, and the cook watched with mouths agape, expecting a hail of slugs through the flimsy door. Instead, the door swung open, and a short, tow-headed young man, who looked to be about nineteen years old, walked out with his hands in the air.

"How'd you find me, deputy?" he asked.

"You shouldn't ask the general store if they's deliver your goods to save you havin' to tote 'em, and you rode right in the middle of the trail. You left a trail a blind man could've followed," Bass said. "Now, hold them hands out 'n let me put handcuffs on 'em."

Tucker, with a downcast look on his face, held his hands out, and Bass slipped the steel cuffs around his wrist and led him to the prisoner wagon.

"Shoot," Henry said. "If I'd known it'd be this easy, I would have stayed home."

Sitting slump-shouldered in the wagon, Tucker gave him a forlorn look. "If I'd knowed it was him comin' after me, I'da saved y'all the trouble 'n jest come down to town and turned myself in."

Bass mounted his horse and pointed it west. "Don't be 'spectin' it to be this easy all the time. It ain't over until we got 'em all trussed up 'n in the wagon. Now, let's move out. We still got four more to find."

They spent the next two days trailing the two land swindlers, who were moving from town to town, always, it seemed, just a few hours ahead of them. The two men, Nathaniel Springer and Jonah Caulfield, had worked together to swindle people in Arkansas and Louisiana out of their land, or convinced them to buy land that didn't exist, and had fled together into Indian Territory when warrants were issued for their arrest. Now, though, they'd split up, complicating the task of following them.

After a day of following overlapping trails, Bass and Henry decided to concentrate on one of the fugitives at a time. They finally tracked Caulfield to an isolated farm, five miles southwest of Shawnee. He'd paid the farmer, a Chickasaw tribesman, for the use of his barn, and was hiding in the hay loft. The man, who knew both Bass and Henry, pointed at the barn when they rode up to his house.

When Bass and Henry walked into the barn and called out his name, he climbed down from the hay loft and meekly surrendered.

It took them another three days to find Springer, who'd shown much more creativity in selecting his hiding place. He had, in fact, hidden in plain sight. Instead of heading for a remote area of the territory, he'd circled around and returned to Shawnee, where he'd paid one of the painted women in the local saloon to allow him to hide under the bed in her room. They literally stumbled upon his hiding place when they entered the saloon to eat lunch, and one of the cleaning women was heard talking to one of the other working girls about 'the strange man hiding in Lulu's room.'

Bass corralled the woman, found out from her where Lulu's room was, signaled Henry to follow him, and the two fo them barged in, lifted the bed, exposing him, and then led the surprised and disappointed Springer out of the saloon in handcuffs.

After Springer's relatively uneventful capture, they only had to find Billy Conner, the young man who'd killed his friend during an argument provoked by a suspicious hand in a card game. The youngest and least experienced of the fugitives they sought, he was also the hardest to find.

While experienced outlaws tend to follow predictable patterns when on the run from the law, Conner had never been in trouble before, had panicked after knifing his friend in an argument over a card game at a local saloon, and had fled into Indian Territory without any kind of plan of escape, only the blind fear of what would happen to him if he was captured. As a result, his movements through the territory were erratic. He would stay in one place for a day or two, and then, for no apparent reason, would leave, heading in a random direction, stopping and sleeping under the stars sometimes, or hiding in barns or abandoned shacks at others.

Tracking him had been like following a wounded coyote, his trail at times doubling back on itself, and with no apparent destination in mind.

But, Bass and Henry were the best trackers in the territory, and they were patient men. Once, during the war, after Bass had run away to the territory, and shortly after they met and became friends, he and Henry had tracked a wounded whitetail deer for three days until they finally cornered it in a blind canyon and put it out of its misery.

They applied this same patience in tracking the young fugitive, and after five days of following one blind trail after another, they'd finally found him, back at the first place they'd picked up his trail, a copse of trees at the south end of a farmer's field, a mile east of Chickasha.

When confronted, he'd pulled out the knife that he'd used on his friend, his only weapon, and waved it wildly at them, screaming that he wouldn't be taken alive. Bass had talked softly to him, all the while edging closer and closer, until he was within reach, whereupon, he'd knocked the blade from the young man's hand with one swipe of one huge hand, and then cuffed him on the side of the head with the other, knocking him unconscious.

When he came to, he was handcuffed, and in the prisoner wagon, sandwiched between the two land swindlers. Bass and Henry stood near the back of the wagon.

"Looks like I figured wrong about how long it'd take to round these fellas up," Bass said.

"I am not complaining," Henry said, smiling. "It means more money for me. It has been a good trip."

Bass removed some folded banknotes from his jacket pocket and counted out the fee he owed his friend. "It was well earned. I'll be seein' you again in a couple of weeks, I reckon."

After counting the bills, folding them, and stuffing them into his pockets, Henry smiled. "I'll be waiting for you. I sure hope the next time's as interesting as this one was."

8.

Belle balanced on the second rail from the bottom of the corral fence, peering at the horses milling around inside the enclosure.

"Looks to be about ten head shy of what you said you were going to get," she said.

Sam Starr, his face glistening with sweat, swung the corral gate shut, and turned to look up at her.

"Yeah, it is," he said. "But, the corral is crowded as you can see. I knew I couldn't get 'em all in there, so I put twelve head up next door at old Joseph Crow's place until the buyer can come look at 'em."

Belle hopped down from the fence.

"I suppose that makes sense. Wouldn't do to crowd 'em up too much and have them hurt each other. That could hurt the sale."

"And, old man Crow ain't chargin' us much to put 'em up for a few days." He clapped his hands. "We're gonna make a good profit off these nags, Belle, a good profit."

She was happy to hear that, for it meant he would probably not be going off on one of his 'trips.' She never asked what he did when he was away from home for days, and he didn't encourage her to ask, nor did he ever talk about what he did. But, she had a good idea what he did, and was sure that it involved relieving other people of their possessions. He was much like his father, and everyone knew that old Tom Starr was a first-class brigand, and in Sam's case, the apple hadn't fallen far from the tree. But, she'd been on that ride before. Her first husband, Jim Reed, like Cole Younger, had been someone she'd known as a teenager. The difference, though, was that she'd had found Reed attractive, and had had a thing for him from the time she was fourteen or fifteen. After the war, when her family moved to Texas, she'd married him. She'd been 18 years old at the time. While Jim had seriously tried farming, it was just too hard, and he'd soon taken up with the Starr clan, involved in stealing whiskey, cattle, and horses in Indian Territory. He'd also thrown in with the James and Younger gangs, and tried his hand at stagecoach robbery, and eight years after they were married, just when she thought she'd convinced him to settle down at the home they had in Paris, Texas, he was shot and killed by an old friend who had betrayed him in order to collect the reward on him for crimes he'd committed from Texas to California.

Six years after Jim Reed's death, she married Sam Starr, and moved to his place in Indian Territory, to live with him and his extended family. Sam had let her name Younger's Bend, despite his concern about her previous relationship with Cole Younger.

Belle knew full well that Sam was still involved in breaking the law, but hoped that he was confining his illegal activities to purloining from the Indians in the territory, so he wouldn't bring the federal law down upon them. The tribal police she felt they could handle with a few well-placed bribes, but the U.S. marshals, especially now that Isaac Parker was the judge in Arkansas, couldn't be easily bribed. And the most feared of all the deputies was her friend, Bass Reeves. Not only could he *not* be bribed, but the man seemed to lead a charmed life. According to the stories Belle heard, he'd been shot at dozens of times, and never been hit, and when he went after a wanted fugitive, that person was as good as behind bars.

She did not, however, share any of her concerns with Sam. She knew that he, like many of the Indians in the territory, respected the dark-skinned lawman, even considered him one of them. But, she worried that if a warrant was ever issued, it would be given to Bass to serve, and that would test the limits of Sam's respect for him.

She had, however, lived among the Cherokee long enough to have adopted some of their philosophy. One of those was, it made no sense to fret over things that you could not control. Better to use your energy to deal with the things staring you in the face. So, she took a deep breath, and looked up at the blue sky, around at the lush green leaves on the trees, and sucked in the air smelling sweet with honeysuckle. What will be, will be, she thought.

Feeling better, she headed for the house to get supper started.

***

That evening, supper done, and the pace of activity around the ranch settled for the evening, Belle and Sam sat on the porch of their ranch house, enjoying the sound of crickets in the reeds along the river and a cool breeze that blew in from the northwest.

Belle was surprised to see a rider approaching from the road. She hadn't expected company so late in the evening. When the rider came into the glow of the lanterns hanging from the porch rafters, she was that it was their neighbor, Joseph Crow. The old man rode hunched over, in the Indian fashion of riding 'small in the saddle' to make yourself a smaller target for an enemy who might be lying in ambush.

He stopped his old gray horse a few feet from the edge of the porch, but didn't dismount.

Sam stood. "Evenin', Joseph," he said. "What brings you over here this late?"

Crow looked nervous, and hesitant. "I hate to bother you, Sam. Evenin', Miz. Belle. It's them horses you left in my corral, Sam. There's a problem."

"Problem? It ain't some kind of sickness, is it?"

Crow shook his head. "No, ain't nothin' like that. It's just . . . well, Sam, after you left, I was muckin' out the stables, 'n I happen to notice a couple of them horses you left with me got brands on 'em I recognize. One belongs to Andrew Crane, 'n one belongs to Sam Campbell. Neither of them white men been selling stock lately, so I was kinda wonderin' how horses with them brands got in with the horses you brought to my place."

"I bought them horses legal from a man up in Muscogee," Sam said. "I got the papers to prove it. You sure you ain't mistaken 'bout them brands?"

"I'm dead sure, Sam. Look, I wouldn't bother you with this, but I can't be caught with no stolen horses on my place, 'specially horses stolen from white men. It's one thing to deal with the tribal council, but this could bring in the federal marshals, 'n you know that ain't no Indian gonna get a break in the white man's court. I hate to ask you this, but can you hold up on sellin' them horses until this can be checked out?"

Sam turned and looked up at Belle, who sat, transfixed, in her chair. She didn't know at that moment what to believe.

"Maybe we should wait, Sam," she said.

"Sure, Belle, honey, we can do that." He turned back to Crow. "Okay, Joseph, you go on home, and don't fret it. I'll take care of this tomorrow."

Crow touched a gnarled finger to the brim of his hat. "I'm much obliged, Sam, much obliged. Let me know what you want to do soon's you can, okay?"

"I'll do that, Joseph. You can count on it."

The old man wheeled his horse around and rode away. Belle sat in her chair, looking at her husband's back, and wondering what was going on, afraid that she knew.

***

The following morning, Belle rose early, not surprised to find Sam's side of the bed empty, for he, too, was habitually an early riser.

She made her way to the kitchen where the cook, a large-breasted Cherokee woman, was preparing a breakfast.

"You see Mr. Sam this morning, Mary?" she asked.

"He ate breakfast already, Miss Belle. Said he had some business to see to."

"Did he say where he was going?"

"No, ma'am, he just said he had business."

Belle felt a cold ache in the pit of her stomach. Sam was up to something, and she had a sinking feeling that that something was not good. There was, however, nothing she could do about it but wait.

She waited until midday, the ache in her stomach turning into a real, hot, stabbing pain. At noon, she found herself standing on the front porch, pacing back and forth, her eyes on the road. She sighed when she saw Sam come riding up the road.

When he rode into the yard, she was still standing there, a worried look on her face.

"Where have you been, Sam?"

He dismounted and walked up onto the porch. "I had some business."

"What kind of business?"

He reached into his coat and pulled out a thick stack of currency. "I sold 'em, Belle, every dang one of 'em, and got top dollar, too."

She gasped. "The horses, you sold the horses? But, you said you'd wait until we sorted out the problem with the brands."

"I know I did, honey, but the buyer wanted 'em right away, and he was payin' good money. Hey, don't fret, it'll be okay."

Somehow, though, she knew that it wouldn't be okay.

9.

Bass suspected the moment that he saw Marshal Fagan waiting at the hitching posts behind the courthouse that something was wrong. As he got closer and saw the pained look on the man's face, he was *certain* that something was wrong.

"Took you a while to get these five, Bass," Fagan said, as Bass dismounted.

"Yeah, that little fella there gave us a run for the money. Had to chase him near all over the territory 'fore we cornered him."

"Other than that, no trouble, I assume?"

Bass hesitated before responding. The question was so out of character for Marshal Fagan, especially in his case, he wondered just how bad things were, or were about to become. Fagan had never questioned him in this manner before.

"No, sir," he said finally. "No trouble. I had to hit the little fella on the head to keep him from hurtin' himself with that pig sticker he carries, but, other than that, everything went fine. You 'spectin' any trouble?"

Now, it was Fagan's turn to hesitate. He tugged at his beard, and seemed to be considering his next words carefully.

"Well, Bass, I reckon it depends on how you look at it. I got one special warrant, and I'd like you to be the deputy to serve it, but I'm wondering how you're gonna take it."

Bass frowned at his boss. "I'll be takin' it just like I do any other warrant you give me, marshal. You want a fugitive brought in, I'll go get him. I don't see no problem."

"The warrant is for Sam and Belle Starr, Bass. They're wanted for larceny."

Bass frowned. "Larceny? What did they do?"

Fagan pulled the folded warrant from his jacket, and studied it for a few seconds.

"The way it was told to me," he said. "Is that they sold a bunch of horses, and among the herd were some stolen animals belonging to a couple of white farmers, named Andrew Crane and Sam Campbell.

"They got proof the horses was stolen?"

"We have affidavits from both of them, and the man that bought the horses from Sam Starr also gave a statement. In addition to that, there's a statement from a neighbor of the theirs, a Cherokee, name of Joseph Crow. Seems Sam put the stolen horses up in Crow's corral because he didn't have room for 'em at his place. Crow witnessed the sale, and he saw and recognized the brands on the stolen horses. I'm afraid we got 'em dead to rights this time, Bass. Are you gonna have a problem serving the warrant? I know you're friendly with 'em, with Belle Starr, at least, and that's why I'd rather it was you make the arrest. Less likely to be gunplay that way."

Bass rubbed at his jaw and locked eyes with Fagan.

"No, marshal," he said. "Ain't gon' be no problem. You want me to bring 'em in, I'll go bring 'em in."

He turned and started to mount.

"No need to go right this minute, Bass. You can wait until tomorrow. Hell, man, you were gone a whole month. Your wife 'n kids got to be missing you something crazy."

Bass paused, his left foot in the stirrup. Finally, he swung his right leg up and over the saddle. He looked down at Fagan.

"Reckon you right 'bout that, marshal. I'll go see to things at home, and head for the territory first thing in the morning."

Without further word, he wheeled his horse around and kicked it into a trot, riding tall in the saddle, heading north toward Van Buren and his family.

Fagan stood by the hitching post, watching as Bass

rode away. The prisoner wagon driver, walked over and stood by him.

"I didn't mean to pry, marshal, but I couldn't help hear what you told him. That's got to be tough, him havin' to arrest Belle Starr. She's just about the best friend he's got in the territory next to Henry Lone Tree. You think he's really gonna being 'em in?"

"Yeah, he'll do it. He won't like it, but Bass Reeves puts the law above everything else. As much as I hated having to give him the job, he's the best man for it."

10.

Belle was dressed for riding, in a dark purple, almost black, velvet riding habit. On her head, she wore a man's homburg with three turkey feathers stuck in the band, and on her feet, her black leather riding boots.

As she headed for the stable to get her horse, Joseph Crow rode into the yard. He rode hunched over in the saddle, with a look of immense sadness on his sun-darkened face.

"Morning, Joseph," she said. "What can I do for you this morning?"

Crow removed his hat, and stared sadly down at her. "Morning, Miss Belle. I come with some bad news."

Sam had ridden into the settlement, claiming he had urgent business to attend to, and her first thought was that he'd gotten into a scrap at the saloon. She hadn't stopped thinking about the horse sale, and the fact that her husband had probably knowingly sold stolen horses. The fact that they'd been stolen from two of the territory's white settlers raised two equally disturbing possibilities; one was that it would attract the attention of the federal authorities in Fort Smith, and the other was the possibility of Crane or Campbell, the owners of the stolen animals, seeking revenge. Of the two situations, the one she feared most was the first. She knew that Sam could take care of himself, and if either man challenged him, there was no doubt who would win in that confrontation. Killing white men would cause trouble, but if they provoked the fight, it was nothing that couldn't be handled. But, if the federal law took an interest, it meant a possible visit from one of the deputy marshals with a warrant for Sam's arrest. She only hoped that if that happened, the deputy wouldn't be her friend, Bass Reeves. Sam being arrested would be bad enough, but to have Bass do it . . . she didn't even want to think about it

"What is the bad news, Joseph?" she asked.

"You remember them horses Sam asked me to put up in my corral? Well, he done sold 'em, you know."

She nodded, worried about where the conversation was going. "Yes, he told me that a few days ago."

"Well, you know I come here and told you 'n him that I saw them brands on a couple of them horses, and I worried they might be stolen. Turns out I was right, 'n Crane and Campbell done gone over to Fort Smith and complained to the U.S. marshal. They think that peckerwood, old Wesley Cotton's the one that stole 'em, 'n he must've sold 'em to Sam. But, Sam's in trouble for sellin' 'em without having legal right to 'em, you know."

Belle's mind churned. At least, it seemed, they weren't accusing Sam of horse stealing, which carried a stiffer penalty—in fact, in some areas, locals didn't even bother calling the law when they caught a horse thief, they just took him to the nearest stout tree limb and gave him a long trip at the end of a short rope.

"I reckon Sam will be in a spot of trouble over that," she said. "I'll tell him when he gets home."

"That ain't all of it, Miss Belle." Crow tugged at the brim of his hat, an expression on his face as if he'd just sucked on a lemon.

Belle slapped her ridding crop against her thigh. "Well, what else is there, Joseph?" she asked, impatiently.

"Well, they done asked me to make a statement; seein' as how Sam put the horses up at my place 'n all. I had to tell 'em I told you 'n him 'bout seein' them suspicious brands on the animals 'fore Sam sold 'em."

"Yes, you did," she said. "How is that a problem?"

"Well, you see, Miss Belle, the marshal, he said that means you knew 'bout the horses bein' stolen, so you are as guilty as Sam. They done issued a warrant for both of you."

Belle suddenly felt a cold stab of fear in her gut.

Because of her long and close association with people on the wrong side of the law, beginning with her first husband and reinforced with her marriage to Sam Starr, Belle was accustomed to people assuming that she was not only aware, but complicit in their crimes. Her association with the likes of the Younger and James gangs only added to the rumors that swirled around her wherever she went. A stylish person by nature, and one who enjoyed the notoriety and attention her stylish dress, sometimes outlandish behavior, and the mystique that came with the title, 'Bandit Queen,' that had been bestowed upon her, she did nothing to either confirm or deny the rumors.

Now, it looked like she would have to pay the price for her pride.

***

Sam didn't return to the ranch until late. Belle had eaten, and left a plate of food on the kitchen table for him, but by the time he rode into the yard, the food was cold. But, Belle, having gone through the chills of fear, was now hot with rage at her husband.

When he walked into the sitting room, she was sitting on the big divan he'd had shipped in from St. Louis for her as a birthday present, a scowl on her face and fire in her eyes.

"Sam, how could you do this to us?" she asked before he could utter a word.

He stood there before her, his hat in his hand, looking at her through narrow slits. "What in blazes you talkin' about, woman? What did I do?"

"You know good and well what you did, Sam Starr. You sold those horses, and you knew some of them were stolen."

His attempt at a look of innocence fell flat.

"Now, Belle, honey, I wasn't sure. The fella I bought 'em from swore up and down he was the rightful owner."

"Did you buy them from one-eyed Wesley Cotton?"

"Uh, yeah, but how'd you know that?"

"It doesn't matter how I know, Sam. You know Wes Cotton's nothing but a mangy horse thief, and a liar."

He cut his eyes away from her, looking down at the floor. She knew he was about to lie. He always avoided looking at her when he lied.

"Honest, Belle," he said. "I didn't know. If I'd thought any of them nags was stolen, I wouldn'ta bought 'em in the first place."

Oh, my Lord, she thought. He *knew* when he bought them that they'd been stolen. We are in a lot of trouble this time.

"You know they got a warrant out for our arrest. They're going to send a marshal after us."

He still avoided looking at her. "Yeah, but they got no proof we did anything wrong."

"That, dear husband, is where you're wrong. They got a statement from the man you sold them to, from the original owner, and Joseph Crow told them he notified us about the brands before you sold them."

"Dang it, I can't believe Joseph would sell me out to the law."

"You can't expect him to lie to them, Sam."

The look on his face told her that he had, in fact, expected just that. The Cherokee culture placed family and clan above all else, so it wasn't considered wrong to lie to authorities to protect a family member or friend. Unfortunately, in the white man's court, such actions were frowned upon.

"Well, what's done is done," he said. "You think maybe we ought to light out and hide until they get tired of lookin' for us?"

"You mean, leave the territory, leave our home? What about the children?"

"We could get my folks to look out for 'em for a spell."

"I suppose we could, but I don't like the idea of going on the run. The marshals won't give up that easy, and, besides, where would we go?"

From the confused look on his face, he apparently hadn't thought it out.

"Well, what are we gonna do?"

"I think we should sleep on it, Sam. Give it some serious thought."

He didn't move. Just stood there with that look on his face that Belle knew meant he had something else to say, and she feared that what he wanted to say was worse than just stolen horses.

"Okay, Sam," she said. "You've got something else on your mind, so spill it."

"Well, I was up at the general store in Puram Gap when I heard about the warrant. I also heard which deputy they're sending to get us."

The cold was back in the pit of her stomach, stabbing like a sharp knife.

"Who?" she asked.

"They're sending Bass Reeves after us, Belle." He smiled. "That's probably good news, you 'n him bein' friends 'n all. Maybe we can talk him into lettin' us go."

She glared at him.

"Sam Starr, you're a bigger fool than I thought. All the times Bass has come here, and you don't know him at all." She turned away from him. "I'm going to bed. I'm going to sleep on this problem."

She knew, though, that she would get no sleep that night.

11.

After breakfast, Bass spent some time parceling out chores to the older children, and then a few minutes with Nellie, reassuring her that on this trip he would be gone only for a few days, because he only had to arrest two fugitives, and both of them lived in the same place. He didn't go into detail about the job, as was his usual practice, not wanting to upset her any more than necessary.

By mid-morning, he was saddled up and on the road to Fort Smith, where he would meet his prison wagon driver and cook. Even though he didn't expect the trip to take more than three days, he believed in being prepared.

He took time for lunch at a small restaurant not far from the courthouse, and by 1:30 in the afternoon, they were on their way.

They were about six miles from Younger's Bend at 5:30, so Bass decided to stop and make camp, preferring to approach the Starr ranch in daylight.

After getting the horses settled, he and John O'Malley, the prison wagon driver, sat around the fire, sipping coffee, while Amos Collins, the cook, prepared supper. Both men had accompanied Bass many times, and an easy-going relationship had developed among them. The two men were among a few whites in Arkansas who didn't object to taking directions from a black man, in fact, they often asked specifically to travel with him because of his practice of trying to arrest fugitives without gunplay.

O'Malley had his hands wrapped around the tin cup, and blew on the hot liquid, his face momentarily obscured by the steam rising from the brown surface.

"I hear we only goin' after two people this time, Bass," he said. "That right?"

Bass blew on his own coffee, and then took a sip. After wiping his mouth, he looked across the cook fire at O'Malley. "Yeah, this is a special job, so we won't be out here very long. Don't worry, though, soon's we get this done, I 'spect I'll be sent out for another month, 'n I'll ask special to have you two come along with me."

Collins stopped stirring the beans, bubbling in the big iron pot, and smiled broadly. "That's sure enough good to hear. I been wantin' to get my roof fixed, so I need the extra money."

"We bein' sent to get just two people," O'Malley said. "They must be pretty special. Who is it?"

Bass made it practice to share all possible information with his crew when they were in the territory. While he'd been lucky, there was always the possibility of a fugitive, or worse, a gang of fugitives, ambushing them. He considered it only fair that the people riding with him knew exactly what risks they were taking.

"We're goin' to arrest Sam and Belle Starr," he said.

O'Malley gaped at Bass. "Whoa, nelly! Ain't they friends of yours?"

"Yeah, I know 'em pretty well.'"

"Man, that's gotta be tough, havin' to arrest a friend. They likely to try and resist?"

Bass rubbed his jaw.

"You know somethin', I pure dee don't know. I sure hope they don't."

***

Bass didn't sleep well that night, and he was uncharacteristically quiet during breakfast. O'Malley and Collins, sensing that he wasn't in the best of moods, also stayed silent. After breakfast, they broke camp and mounted up.

Six miles went by rapidly, over rolling farm land with well-tended fields, and small herds of cattle and horses.

The Starr ranch was one of the most prosperous in the area known as Younger's Bend, named, Bass had learned, for the outlaw Cole Younger, a guerilla during the war who had turned to a life of crime after the war ended. The Youngers and Belle's family had known each other in Missouri where Belle was born, and she apparently still held the Younger clan in high esteem.

All was quiet as they rode into the front yard.

Sam Starr walked out onto his front porch just as Bass dismounted.

"Mornin', Bass," he said.

"Mornin', Sam," Bass said. "Reckon you know why I'm here."

"Yeah, I heard."

"You not plannin' on givin' me no trouble, I hope."

Starr raised his hands. "Nope, no trouble from me," he said. "I'll go in peaceable like. I got no desire to see if you're as good with them shootin' irons as I hear."

Bass smiled ruefully. "Is Miss Belle here? The warrant includes her, too."

Starr looked puzzled.

"Tell you the truth, Bass, I got no idea where Belle is. She was here when we went to bed last night, but when I woke up this mornin', she was gone."

"Runnin' don't seem like her," Bass said.

"Naw, naw it don't. I don't know what to tell you, Bass. I got no idea where she went to."

One part of Bass's mind was relieved that she wasn't there. He hadn't really looked forward to having to arrest her. But, another part worried. What had she done?

12.

As Bass helped Sam Starr into the back of the prison wagon, after having gotten the man's agreement that he wouldn't try to escape, a woman wearing a black velvet riding habit, a man's hat with peacock feathers atop her flowing brown hair, rode up to the hitching rail in front of the federal court building in Fort Smith, Arkansas.

Passersby gawked at her, but she paid them no mind as she slipped from the saddle and tied her horse to the rail. After adjusting her hat, and smoothing the wrinkles out of her riding habit, she strode regally up the walk to the marble steps leading up to the big double doors.

When she pushed the doors open and entered the reception foyer, the clerk on duty at the reception desk at the foot of the stairs gaped in astonishment. This was not the usual type of lady seen in the court, but someone important.

"Uh, can I help you, ma'am?" he asked.

"Yes, I would like to speak with Marshal John Fagan," she said.

"Yes, ma'am, and can I tell the marshal who wants to see him?"

"Starr, Belle Star."

The man's mouth dropped open, and he stood as if rooted to the floor. She stood in front of the desk, tapping the toe of her riding boot against the floor.

"Well," she said. "Are you going to tell the marshal I'm here?"

The clerk reacted as if she'd slapped him. "Oh, yes, ma'am. You wait right here. I'll go let the marshal know you want to see him."

Glancing back over his shoulder, he rushed past the stairs, to the hallway leading to Fagan's first-floor office.

The lobby at that time of day wasn't very busy, with only a few people coming and going. But, each person who walked through the space slowed down to gaze at the woman in her fancy dress standing near the reception desk.

A few minutes after his departure, the clerk returned, followed by an impressive looking man, wearing a dark blue jacket with a U.S. marshal's badge over the left breast.

The man extended a hand as he neared Belle. "Miz Starr, I'm Marshal Fagan," he said. "I understand you wanted to speak to me?"

She shook his hand, firmly, like her father had taught her to do.

"That's right, marshal. I understand that you have a warrant for my arrest?"

"Uh, yes, Miz Starr, as a matter of fact, we do."

"In that case, sir," she said. "I am here to surrender." She held her hands out, wrists bared.

After a second of shocked hesitation, Fagan held his hand up. "That won't be necessary, ma'am," he said. "I'll escort you to a cell."

The clerk, mouth wide open, watched as Fagan led her away.

Within the hour, first the courthouse, and then the whole town, was abuzz with the news that the Bandit Queen, Belle Starr, had turned herself in to the law, and was now in jail.

A crowd gathered in front of the courthouse building, and just stood there quietly gazing at the corner that held the jail where federal prisoners were held awaiting trial. Fagan called in several deputies to guard the entrances to the building, but the crowd made no move to enter.

Two deputies, standing near the main entrance, looked out at the silent crowd. "Can you believe it," one said. "All these people out there, gazing at this building like we got some kinda saint inside or something."

"She might be an outlaw," the other said. "But, lots of folks round these parts admire this Belle Starr. You know, she's a friend of Bass Reeves."

"Yeah, I heard that. Wonder if he knew she was an outlaw?"

"No, I doubt it. You know Bass. Hell, that man would arrest his own son if he broke the law. He's got a stick up his back about that. Reckon he's gonna be mighty put out, though."

13.

Bass was less put out than confused.

He'd been surprised, but somewhat pleased, when, upon his return to Fort Smith, he'd been informed by the clerk at reception in the court building that none other than Belle Starr had turned herself in to the law, and was at that moment residing in a cell in the detention wing of the building.

He was upset at his friend being in jail, but relieved that she'd not decided to go on the run, which would have made her a wanted fugitive, in the gunsights of every marshal, town sheriff, and bounty hunter within five hundred miles, some of whom would have no qualms about shooting a woman, despite the warrant not stating that she was wanted 'dead or alive.'

Bass considered visiting her in her cell, but decided that it might be misunderstood, so, after depositing Sam Starr and the required paperwork, which he'd had O'Malley complete for him, he checked in with Marshal Fagan, learned that he had no warrants available, and that none would be forthcoming for another day or two, went home to his family.

After an initial arraignment, a grand jury brought indictments against both Belle and Sam for larceny in relation to the sale of stolen property, although the U.S. Attorney had sought one for horse theft, a more serious offense. They were allowed to return to Younger's Bend to await a decision on a scheduled trial date.

Despite a reputation for dispensing speedy justice, U.S. Court Judge Isaac Parker scheduled Belle and Sam's trials for November, to give them time to prepare their defense against the charges that had been filed. This also gave Bass time for a month-long trip back into the territory, enabling him to fulfill his promise to

O'Malley and Collins, to make up for the all-too-short trip to arrest Sam. They returned after twenty-eight days with ten fugitives shackled in the prisoner wagon, and the prospect of over three thousand dollars in reward money for Bass. The joyous homecoming he received helped him to overcome his sadness at his friend having to stand before Judge Parker and answer for charges that Bass was convinced she was innocent of.

There was a chill in the air on the first day of the trial of the United States versus Sam Starr and Belle Starr. Parker's courtroom was packed, with some people shoving in and standing against the wall in the back, despite the deputy marshals trying to keep them out. Finally, to avoid a riot, Marshal Fagan allowed several people to enter, provided they remained quiet and orderly. He and Bass, along with four other deputies, took seats in the back row in order to be able to watch the entrance as well as the entire courtroom

A quiet murmur began when the defendants were led in by two deputy marshals, accompanied by their attorney.

The murmur cut off abruptly when the bailiff said, "All rise for his honor, Judge Isaac Parker."

Parker entered the courtroom from his antechamber behind the elevated bench from which he presided. In his black robe, his white hair and beard enveloping his face, he looked to Bass like an avenging angel. He wore a stern expression as he seated himself, reinforcing the impression people had of him. Isaac C. Parker, the 'Hanging Judge,' as he'd come to be known since being appointed to preside over the Western District of Arkansas and the Indian Territories by President U.S. Grant, had sentenced dozens of defendants in capital cases to hang. But, contrary to his reputation, he opposed the death penalty, and had told a northern reporter who interviewed him that, when a jury found a defendant guilty in a capital case, because the death penalty was mandatory, he had no choice but to impose it. This distinction, though, was lost on the common folks in the territory. They took the nickname to imply that Parker was a harsh judge, and feared coming before him as much as they feared having Bass Reeves on their tail.

Bass looked up at the man who had hired him as a deputy, and saw what others failed to see. Presiding over the largest and busiest court in the entire judicial system was beginning to take its toll. Parker looked tired. Holding court, often as long as sixteen hours per day, five days a week, had robbed a once vibrant man of his vitality. To Bass, he looked like someone sorely in need of rest.

Despite his physical appearance, he still maintained iron control over his courtroom, and immediately opened the proceedings, instructing the prosecuting attorney to begin presenting his case.

No expert in the courtroom aspects of the law, Bass was nonetheless impressed with the way the U.S. attorney piled fact on top of fact, as he presented what, even to Bass, seemed like an iron-clad case against Sam and Belle, who sat stone-faced and silent as the proceedings got underway.

Witness after witness, under the gentle, but persistent questioning of the prosecutor, swore that Sam Starr had been in possession of horses that had been stolen from Andrew Crane and Sam Campbell. Both men showed papers proving ownership of the horses and question, and provided details about discovering that the animals had been stolen just days before Sam Starr sold them to a buyer from Texas. The Texan, when called to the stand, asserted that he'd purchased the horses from Sam Starr, pointing at him as he spoke, and had been assured that the title to them was free and clear.

The damning evidence, though, came from Joseph Crow. Though he seemed reluctant to speak, under the prosecutor's prodding, he stated that he had informed Sam and Belle that he'd recognized the brands on a couple of the horses Sam had left at his place, and that he'd informed them he believed the animals to be stolen. When he said that both of them had assured him that the sale of the horses would be delayed until the claim could be investigated, but that Sam had come to his ranch the following day with a buyer and disposed of the horses, there were audible gasps from several members of the jury.

Throughout the testimony of prosecution witnesses, Sam and Belle kept their gaze on the table behind which they sat.

Finally, the prosecutor, stood and looked up at the judge. "Your honor," he said. "The prosecution rests."

Parker pointed his gavel at the defense attorney.

"Counselor, are you ready to present your case?" he asked.

"Uh, I suppose so, your honor," the man said.

"Very well, present your first witness."

"Uh, well, your honor, I don't have any witnesses."

Parker's eyes blazed. "You just said you're ready to present your case," he roared. "How are you going to do that if you have no witnesses?"

"I will present my case in my closing remarks, your honor. My clients acted in good faith, and should be acquitted."

His face wrinkled and his lips pursed as if he'd sucked on a half-ripe lemon, Parker glared down at the man. When he spoke, his disgust was apparent.

"I can't tell you how to run your case, young man," he said. "But, if that's the way you want to do it, so be it. It's your funeral, or rather, it's your clients' future you're playing with here." His gaze switched to the prosecutor. "Counselor, you may present your closing argument."

With a look that was a mixture of surprise and smug satisfaction, the prosecutor stood and gave a subdued, but damning oration of the evidence he'd presented, the statements from witnesses that proved beyond doubt that the defendants had knowingly sold property that did not belong to them, and that the defense had not presented one shred of evidence to refute that charge. He piled on by pointing out that Sam Starr was the leader of the notorious Starr clan, known throughout the Indian Territory for their unlawful acts against the various tribes there, and Belle Starr's reputation as the Bandit Queen, who had previously consorted with a known Texas criminal before marrying Starr. "Therefore," he said, in conclusion. "You gentlemen of the jury have no alternative but to find the defendants guilty of the charges as set forth in the indictment." With a last smile of triumph, he sat.

The defense attorney was far less eloquent. He pointed out that his clients had not stolen anything, nor were they accused of stealing. They had been, he asserted, victimized by the true thief, and had bought and sold the horses in good faith. He excoriated the prosecutor for bringing up rumor and innuendo which had no bearing on the case, in an effort to prejudice the jury against his clients. "Gentlemen of the jury," he said. "What you have here is a situation in which my clients made a mistake, an unwise, but honest mistake. They trusted the man who sold them the horses, and then sold them with no intent of malice. I would ask that you ignore the prosecutor's salacious remarks about them, his slanderous words that were designed to make you view them in a most unfavorable light. I maintain that, despite the parade of witnesses the prosecution brought before you, he has not proven beyond reasonable doubt that my clients knowingly committed any crime, and I ask you to do the right thing, find them not guilty."

The courtroom fell silent when he sat down, his shoulders slumped. Bass could see that his words had not had any impact on the jury, who, as a man, stared at Sam and Belle as if they were being accused of murder.

Parker sent the jury into deliberation with an injunction to ignore the prosecutor's remarks about the defendants' reputations, and to decide the case based solely upon the evidence presented. When the jury had filed out of the courtroom, Parker called a recess. No one moved. Everyone had come to see the show, and weren't about to risk losing their front row seats. Parker shrugged, stood, and went into his chambers. Deputies moved to the front of the room and escorted the defendants to a holding area down the hall from the courtroom where they would wait for the jury to decide their fate.

They didn't have long to wait.

Thirty minutes after departing the courtroom, the jury was back. The room was abuzz with hushed conversations as everyone waited for Judge Parker to return. When he finally appeared, and called the court back into session, as hush fell over the space like a blanket. All eyes were on the twelve men sitting in the jury box.

"The defendants will rise." Slowly, Belle and Sam stood, and faced the jury. "Gentlemen of the jury," he said. "Have you reached a verdict?"

The jury foreman stood. "Yes, we have, your honor."

"How say you?"

"Your honor, we the jury, find the defendants, Sam Starr and Belle Starr, guilty as charged."

Parker banged his gavel to silence the loud conversations that immediately erupted.

"Order, I'll have order in this courtroom, or it'll be cleared," he thundered. "Mister foreman, was this a unanimous verdict?"

"It was, your honor."

"Then, I thank you for your service." He turned his steely gaze upon the defendants. "Ordinarily," he said.

"I would take a few days to determine sentencing, but in this case, I have already decided." He paused and cleared his throat. Everyone leaned forward on their seats, their eyes upon him as he frowned at Sam and Belle. "While what you've done is serious, I'm taking into account that this is your first conviction, so I am sentencing each of you to one year in the Federal House of Corrections in Detroit, Michigan, and I hope that upon completion of your sentences you will decide to become decent citizens."

Belle and Sam shared incredulous looks, while the prosecutor and the defense lawyer each looked stunned, albeit for different reasons. The courtroom was silent for several heartbeats, except for the ticking of the clock on the wall near the entrance.

Finally, Parker banged his gavel and broke the silence. "This court is adjourned," he said.

He stood, and in a flurry of his black robe, departed the courtroom. Deputies moved to take charge of the prisoners, who would be moved back to the detention center where they would be prepared for their move from Arkansas to Detroit. Bass and Marshal Fagan, after looking around and ascertaining that there would be no disorder, left the courtroom and walked downstairs to Fagan's office.

Once inside the office, Fagan immediately pulled a stack of warrants from his desk.

"I reckon you'll be wanting to head back to the territory right away," he said.

Bass's head bobbed up and down. "Reckon I will, marshal, reckon I will."

14.

Responding to a petition from the defense attorney, Judge Parker delayed Belle's transfer to the prison in Detroit by a month to allow her to make arrangements for the custody and care of her children while she served her sentence.

In the meantime, Bass went back into the territory to arrest a group of fugitives, including a band of five cattle rustlers who'd been operating out of a hideout near Durant, across the Red River into northeast Texas, where they conducted nighttime raids on small ranches and farms.

He had just returned, and was signing the captured men over to the jailer, when a guard at the detention center informed him that Belle Starr had asked to speak with him as soon as possible.

He found her, sitting on the edge of the wooden bunk, in a cell in the far corner of the holding area. Time in prison had taken its toll. Her brown hair hung lank around her face. Her once vibrant eyes were dulled, and her complexion was sallow. In addition, subsisting on jail food had added pounds to her frame, giving her a dowdy appearance, and her clothing, usually immaculate, was wrinkled, making her look like a cleaning woman just completing a long work shift.

When Bass appeared at her cell door, she looked up at him with a haunted look in her eyes. To Bass, she had the look of a thoroughly beaten woman.

"Bass, thank you for coming," she said. "I was afraid that, under the circumstances, you might not."

"Now, why would I do that, Miz Belle? This don't change the fact that you and me are friends."

Her eyes glistened with unshed tears. "What did I do to deserve a friend like you, Bass?"

"It ain't what you done, so much as what you are. You always been nice to me, not treatin' me no different than any other person. Oh, and I surely do like the way you plays the piano."

She smiled, and stood. Walking to the bars, she grasped them and placed her forehead against the cold metal.

"There's something I want you to know," she said. "We didn't steal those horses . . . or at least, I didn't."

"I never believed you did. But, I don't understand why you didn't speak up at the trial, tell them that you didn't have nothin' to do with it."

She shook her head. "It's complicated, Bass. See, I did know the horses were probably stolen. I was sitting right there when Joseph Crow told us." Bass started to speak, but she held her hand up to stop him. "No, I know what you're going to say, and I know that Sam said he'd wait on the sale, but I should've known better. Sam saw all that money, and couldn't resist, and I should have known that. So, in that sense, I guess I'm as guilty as he is, because I didn't stop him."

"You shouldn't be goin' to jail for *not* doin' something. If you didn't break the law, you're innocent."

He placed a large dark hand on her fingers gripping the bars. She smiled. "I'm not exactly innocent, Bass. Oh, I never stole a horse, or robbed a bank, but I've done a few bad things, so I guess I have to pay for them."

"You gon' be okay in prison?"

"I can survive," she said. "They let me take care of my children, and I'll be able to take some clothes and personal things. It's only a year. I'll make it."

"If there's anything you need, anything I can do, you just let me know."

She reached through the bars and patted his hand. "Just stay my friend, Bass Reeves. That's all I can ask. Now, the marshals will be taking me to the train station in a while. It'd probably be better for both of us if you weren't here, so I'll say goodbye. You take care of yourself, Bass Reeves."

"You, too, Belle Starr," he said.

She turned away and went back to the cot. She sat and began packing her belongings.

Bass turned and began the long walk down the corridor to the freedom outside the dank cells. He never looked back.

Renegade Roundup

1.

By the time they arrived in the Chickasaw Nation Bass Reeves and his entourage had six fugitives chained in one of the two prisoner wagons he'd brought along on this trip past the deadline, that imaginary line in the dirt some eighty miles west of Fort Smith, beyond which deputy marshals were warned by the fugitives who hid out in Indian Territory that if it was crossed their lives were forfeit. Bass had made many trips across that line and had yet to lose in an encounter with any outlaw foolhardy enough to go up against him.

Two of his three posse men, Jake Stern, a stoop-shouldered farmer who worked a small holding not far from Bass's farm near Van Buren, Arkansas, and Alvin Steadman, a half-breed white who was part Cherokee, but who preferred not to live in the territory with his tribe, had been urging him to take the six men they'd already captured back to the federal jail in Fort Smith, as they were quickly approaching the month that such trips normally took. The third, an old friend from his days in the territory, during the War of Southern Insurrection when he'd run away from Texas and his abusive master, Colonel George Reeves of the 11th

Texas Cavalry, right after the Battle of Pea Ridge in March 1862, Joseph Lone Tree, a full-blood Cherokee, by whose side he'd fought in Cherokee Chief Opotheyahola's pro-Union cavalry brigade during the war, and who often accompanied him on his forays into Indian Territory, kept silent. Henry knew Bass well and knew that when he set his mind to something, there was no turning him away from it.

"Look, you fellas," Bass said. "I got me warrants here for the Dawkins gang, and we ain't goin' back to Forth Smith until all six of 'em is chained in that there empty wagon."

"Couldn't we just take these ones in, take a few days to rest, and come back for Dawkins and his yahoos?" Stern asked. "My rump's plumb sore from bein' in the saddle for near on to a month now."

"Naw, we ain't puttin' it off to next trip. Now, quite your belly achin', and let's get on in to town and see if somebody can tell us where to find 'em."

Henry chuckled as Bass wheeled his horse and headed off down the road. As stubborn as a mule, that Bass is, he thought, and with them big fists of his, when he hits a man, it feels like he been kicked by a mule. At six-foot-two and weighing nearly two hundred pounds, Bass was far bigger than the average man, and could whip any two people in a fair fight. His prowess with rifle and hand gun, in either hand, was known throughout Arkansas and the Indian Territory, and since he'd been a young slave boy, butler, bodyguard, and valet to old man William Reeves, father of George, he'd been taught to use weapons, and had such a natural feel for them, the old man had entered him in turkey shoots and other shooting competitions from the time he was a teenager, and he'd won them all against competitors, black and white. He was so good, in fact, that around Van Buren, he'd been banned from entering competitions on the grounds that it was unfair to all the other competitors.

Bass, in the eyes of his friend, was like a tornado, a force of nature that you didn't want to get crosswise to.

When they rode into Tishomingo, one of the main towns in the lands owned and controlled by the Chickasaw tribe, the sight of a wagon with six chained fugitives staring through the bars brought most of the residents out into the streets to gawk and point. Bass rode in front, looking for a sheriff's office where he could make enquiries as to the whereabouts of the Dawkins gang.

When he saw the town hall, a two-story wood frame building sandwiched between a funeral home and a saloon, he decided that it would do. A town official should know what was going on.

"Y'all wait here," he said as he dismounted. "I'm goin' inside and see if they knows where we might find Dawkins and his men."

While Henry, the other two posse men, and Harvey Jackson, the cook, saw to the animals and prisoners, Bass rode across the street to the town hall. He dismounted and secured his black stallion to the hitching rail.

Except for a slump-shouldered, balding man of middle years, his shirt sleeves rolled up his scrawny arms almost to his elbows, sitting at a large desk piled high with documents of various sizes and thicknesses, the reception area of the building was empty. The ceiling was high, and the two large windows in the front of the building let in sufficient light, but the man still had a coal oil lantern on his desk, which struck Bass as a dangerous practice, given the untidy state of the paper scattered around the lantern. Bass had expected to find an Indian in the town hall, not a white man, but he'd noticed that more and more whites were settling in the territory, and many of the tribes, despite the shabby treatment they'd historically received from whites, accepted them.

He approached the desk but kept back about four

feet, figuring there was no sense taking the chance that the man wouldn't accidently tip the lantern over and set the whole room ablaze. The man was peering intently at a map, his fingers tracing the irregular lines drawn upon it. Bass waited patiently for half a minute, occasionally scraping the toe of his boot against the hardwood floor to get the man's attention.

Finally, he cleared his throat.

"Excuse me, mister," he said. "I hate to interrupt you, but I need some information."

The man looked up, regarding Bass with watery blue eyes.

"Oh, sorry, stranger," he said. "I didn't hear you come in. What you want to know?"

Bass pulled the warrant for the Dawkins gang from his coat pocket and put it on the desk. "That there's a federal warrant for the arrest of Clint Dawkins and the members of his gang. They's wanted for cattle rustling and a whole bunch of other things. I heard they might be operatin' here in Chickasaw Nation."

The man picked the warrant up and held it close to his face. When he put it down, he looked up at Bass, a frown on his face.

"Can't rightly say I know 'em or have heard anything about 'em. 'Course I doubt they'd be comin' to a place like Tishomingo, 'specially if they's tryin' to unload stolen livestock."

"You got any idea where I might start lookin' for 'em?"

"Well now, you might look over Fort Sill way. The purchasing agent for the army there ain't too particular where goods come from. Could be, if they're selling stolen cattle, they'd head over that way."

Bass hadn't thought of that possibility, but it made sense. It wasn't uncommon for the civilian traders who made purchases on behalf of the government to cut corners in order to maximize their own profits.

"That ain't a bad idea," he said. "I reckon we'll

mosey on over that way."

"So, you're a deputy marshal, are you?" the man asked, despite Bass's badge being displayed prominently on his coat. "Do you only go after outlaws you got a warrant for?"

"No, it's our job to enforce the law, so if we run into some galoot breaking the law, we have to take him in."

"Well, we got ourselves one of the biggest and meanest outlaws in the territory right here in Chickasaw Nation. Would you be interested in going after him?"

"That depends. Who is he, and what's he done?"

"He's a Seminole, goes by the name of Greenleaf. As to what he's done, well, there ain't much he ain't done. Mostly, though, he runs whiskey from Texas into the nation, but he also does a little robbery and murder."

While it wasn't a high priority, the deputy marshals were charged with trying to stem the flow of liquor into Indian Territory. Robbery and murder, on the other hand, made this a higher priority case.

"Who's he done kilt, and when?" Bass asked.

"Word is he done killed and robbed a mail rider over near Fort Washita a few days ago."

"In that case, I'm plumb interested in gettin' him. You know where he might be found?"

"Right at the moment, no," the man said. "But, I hear he's bringin' in a load of whiskey today or tomorrow. He sells the stuff out of a compound over near Ardmore."

Bass thought about it. This would delay getting the Dawkins crew, but the killing of a mail rider was serious business. His own group wouldn't be too happy at the time this would add to this trip, but, he thought, the law's the law.

"I reckon we'll ride on over to Ardmore and see if we can find this here Greenleaf fella," he said.

2.

Just as he'd anticipated, Stern and Steadman grumbled at the extra time away from their families going after Greenleaf would mean, but when Bass announced that this also meant more money in their pockets, as they were being paid three dollars a day, they quieted down. Jackson informed Bass that he would need to stop at the general store and buy a few extra supplies for the added time, and Henry simply nodded.

After the extra rations were stowed away in the cook wagon, they set out for Ardmore, located about thirty miles west of Tishomingo. It was nearing dark when they arrived on the outskirts of the town.

"Y'all get the horses to the livery stable," he said to Stern and Steadman. "And I'll see if the local sheriff can house our prisoners for the night."

"What if he won't?" Stern asked.

"Then, we guard 'em while they sleep in the livery stable with the animals."

It turned out that Stern's pessimism was right. The local jail, according to the deputy who was on evening duty, was filled to capacity after a donnybrook at a local saloon, so they made arrangements with the owner of the livery stable to chain the six prisoners in an empty stall, and they took turns guarding them, while the rest of the crew slept outside on saddle blankets under the wagons.

The next morning, Bass went back to the sheriff's office to get directions to the compound where Greenleaf allegedly kept the whiskey he brought into the area.

The sheriff, a tall, broad-shouldered man with a white mustache that drooped past his lower lips, welcomed Bass to his office.

"What kin I do fer you, deputy?" he asked.

"I'm looking for an outlaw, name of Greenleaf," Bass replied. "I was hopin' you might be able to tell me where I might find him."

"You ain't plannin' to go up agin that injun by yerself, are you?"

"Well now, that kinda depends on the situation. I got me three posse men with me, though."

The sheriff shook his head.

"Four of you agin Greenleaf and his four galoots. You don't stand a chance. That there Seminole is one mean cuss. I hear he done kilt five or six men, some of 'em for just lookin' at him crooked, but most he kilt to rob 'em."

"Why ain't you arrested him, sheriff?"

"Well now, deputy, he ain't done none of these things in my town, so it ain't my problem. 'Sides, I only got me two deputies, and they's just about fit to mind the jail at night or to break up a fight between drunks at the local saloons. Ain't no way we gonna go up agin Greenleaf, and if you was smart, you'd keep ridin', too."

"I can't do that. I got a sworn duty to uphold the law. Now, can you tell me where I might find him?"

Shaking his head, the sheriff gave Bass directions to Greenleaf's place, a fenced-in compound just north of town and off the main road about half a mile.

Bass left Steadman and Jackson to guard the prisoners and took Henry and Stern to get a look at the layout.

The trail leading in from the main road was little more than two lines in the grass, made by wagons traveling the same route for who knew how many years. Tall evergreens lined the trail as it wound up a slight hill. At the top, it dipped down into a bowl of a valley, in the center of which was a high rail fence surrounding a one-story wood-frame house and a barn. An empty wagon sat next to the barn.

They dismounted and tied their horses to some

hardwood saplings in the trees, and crept hunched over to peer at the compound from behind a clump of ivy vines.

"Looks like he done already delivered the whiskey," Stern said. "We goin' down to arrest him now, Bass?"

Bass scanned the compound. Other than one man with a rifle on his lap, sitting on a chair on the porch of the house, there didn't seem to be any guards. But, as he well knew, there would be other armed men around, and the last thing he wanted was a gun battle.

"Naw, I think we oughta wait until they settle in for the night," he said. "We'll let 'em get good and asleep, and then we move in."

"Just the three of us?"

"If they's all sleepin', it won't take but the three of us."

3.

Waiting, when there's nothing to do but sit and listen to the clicking, whistling, chirping, and hooting of night creatures, is difficult for most people. It certainly was for Stern, who mumbled to himself and fidgeted during the entire evening as they sat in the thick ivy vines watching Greenleaf's compound, from first dark until the sky began to get the first tinges of purplish-gray, signaling that dawn was imminent. Bass and Henry, accustomed to sitting quietly for hours during reconnaissance missions during the war, and on hunting trips after, sat cross-legged, their forearms resting on their thighs, and simply waited.

Finally, Bass sensed that the people in the compound would be in the last stages of sleep, probably dreaming, and any guard would be either asleep or drowsy. He rose in a fluid motion and brushed off the seat of his trousers.

"Time to go," he said.

"About time," Stern said. "My backside was gettin' all cramped up sittin' here on this cold ground. I don't know how the two of you do it."

"Well, git the cramps out and lets git movin'."

"Are we going through the front gate?" Henry asked.

"Naw, that things looks like it'll screech like an old owl. I reckon we just hoist ourselves over the fence."

"Aw, jeez," Stern said. "First, I gotta sit here all night and git all cramped up, and now I gotta go climb over a rail fence. Bass, you sure don't make these trips easy on a fella, I'll tell you that."

Bass laughed quietly. Stern complained about everything, but he always did what he was asked to do. "Goin' over the fence and not gettin' shot at is a mite better than the other way 'round, don't you reckon?"

"Yeah, I s'pose so. Aw, let's git this over with."

The three men made their way slowly to a point at the fence off to the side where there wasn't a clear view from the house, just in case the guard was on the porch and wasn't sleeping. As usual, Bass went first, pulling himself up and over the fence with ease. Henry followed, and then came Stern, who stumbled to his knees and had to put his hand over his mouth to smother the curse that came when his knees hit the hard ground.

Bass pulled his Colt Peacemaker and motioned for Henry and Stern to do the same. He put a finger to his lips and began moving toward the house.

They moved in single file, Bass leading and Stern following Henry. When they reached the house, Bass edged along the wall and peeked around the corner. As he suspected, the lone guard was slumped in a chair, his rifle on his lap, snoring loudly. He tapped Henry on the shoulder and pointed at the guard. Henry slipped past him as silent as a shadow, crouching low until he was in front of the sleeping guard. He then stepped up onto the porch. The loose boards made a creaking sound. The guard jerked awake and made a sniffing sound just as the butt of Henry's rifle slammed into his head. He slumped back in the chair, no longer snoring. Henry turned and waved Bass and Stern forward.

"He's gonna have a powerful headache when he wakes up," Stern said, looking down at the unconscious man.

"Hush up," Bass whispered. "You gon' wake 'em up inside the house."

He might as well have saved his warning. He eased the door open, and the three of them stepped inside. The room they entered was a large sitting room, but sparsely furnished. A ragged old sofa sat in the center, fronted by a rough-wood carved low table, upon which sat four empty whiskey bottles. A man lay sprawled on the sofa, his mouth open, and a line of spittle trailing down his chin. Off to his left, another man lay in a heap on the floor, his thumb in his mouth, and making snorting noises through his nose.

"Don't neither one of them look like this fella Greenleaf," Bass whispered. "Get 'em trussed up, and I'll go look for him."

He walked carefully across the room, but neither of the sleeping men noticed. There were two doors at the far side. Through the open one Bass could see into the kitchen, with pots, pans, and dishes stacked haphazardly on a table in the center, but otherwise empty. The other was closed, and he assumed that it led to a bedroom.

He was right. He opened the door and slipped into a large room, about the same size as the sitting room. A brass rail bed in the far corner, with a body draped over the covers, face down, snoring loudly, one boot on, the other lying on its side beside the bed. A whiskey bottle on its side on the floor, some of its contents having leaked and left a large, irregular dark stain on the wood floor.

Bass could see the left side of the sleeping man's face, and from the description he'd been given recognized him as the notorious Seminole outlaw, Greenleaf.

He walked across the room and put the tip of the barrel against the man's cheek.

"Time to wake up, sleepy head," he said.

Greenleaf's eyes blinked open and his body stiffened. "Wha-, who, how in hell did you git in here?"

"Why, I just walked through the door. I would've knocked, but everybody was sleepin'. Now, haul your carcass outa that there bunk. I'm placin' you under arrest."

Greenleaf blinked again, and slowly rolled over until he was lying on his back, his eyes crossed as Bass placed the business end of the Colt on the bridge of his nose.

"Who in the blazes are you?"

"Allow me to introduce myself," Bass said. "I'm Bass Reeves, deputy United States marshal out of Fort Smith, Arkansas. You, I take it, are Greenleaf, bootlegger, thief, and murderer?"

The Seminole growled something unintelligible.

"I'll take that as a yes. Now, set up so's I can put the irons on you."

4.

With Greenleaf and his three confederates in chains and in the wagon with the six other prisoners, Bass set out in earnest to locate Clint Dawkins and his gang.

Taking the advice of the sheriff, Bass concentrated on the trails heading west, especially those that terminated at Fort Sill, the cavalry installation in the southeastern region of what was being called Oklahoma Territory. Troopers of the Tenth Cavalry were currently among those stationed there, and the purchasing agents who provided supplies to the colored soldiers had, Bass knew, slightly more tendency to cut corners than did those buying for other units. It made sense that if Dawkins had cattle to unload, that would be the place to go.

They searched for two days, checking every dry wash, box canyon, and hidden pasture, asking at farms, ranches, small settlements, and growing towns, but kept coming up dry. A few times, people told them that they'd seen a bunch of men driving a herd of cattle, but each time, when Bass questioned them, the stories fell apart. Either the number of drovers didn't match the number he knew were in the Dawkins gang, or they included Mexican and colored cowboys, and he knew that everyone in the Dawkins gang was white.

Each time they hit a dry hole, Stern's grumbling about wanting to go home got louder. Bass shut his mind to the muttering and kept looking. He was determined that every member, every live member depending upon whether or not they decided to shoot it out, would be in a prisoner wagon when he returned to Fort Smith from this trip.

In the evening of the second day, as they were looking for a suitable place to camp for the night, they met a lone rider, slumped in the saddle, heading east.

"Howdy, stranger," Bass said. "Wherebouts you

bound?"

A middle-aged man with stringy brown hair that hung loosely beneath his Stetson, and a scraggly mustache, he eyed Bass with a guarded, but not unfriendly look.

"I'm on my way to Muskogee," he said. "Old rancher over that way needs a new foreman, and he offered me the job. I'se down to my last dime, and sweepin' saloons in Lawton, so I figgered, why not."

"Muskogee is a nice little town. Say, you didn't happen to pass a gang of men drivin' a herd of cows, did you?"

"Matter of fact, I did. Yestiddy, when I'se lookin' for a place to camp for the night, I run into this buncha cowpokes, 'bout five or six of 'em, with a herd. They's camped 'bout fifty mile east of here. Right unfriendly bunch they was, too. Didn't like me campin' near 'em and wouldn't even share their coffee with a stranger."

"Now, that's downright mean. We was just about to stop and make camp ourselves," Bass said. "You welcome to bunk down with us, and we'd be happy to share our food and coffee."

"Now, that's the kind of hospitality a man expects on the trail. Don't mind iffen I do."

They found a clearing in a stand of pines just off the road with a shallow, but clear spring not far away, and set up camp. The prisoners were chained to the wheels of the wagons, and Steadman was assigned the first guard shift. Jackson got a fire started, and very soon had hot cups of coffee in everyone's hand—except for the prisoners, who were forced to wait until the food was ready to get anything other than water to drink.

Over coffee, the rider, Deke Johnson, added details to his encounter with the cattle herders, some of which Bass discounted as the natural tendency of lonely men to embroider tales with each telling, but other details rang true, so he added them to his store of knowledge about the Dawkins gang.

He learned, for instance, that Clint Dawkins doted on his younger brother, Billy, who he was grooming to be leader of the gang when he himself got too old to handle the rigors of the job. He also learned that both Dawkins appeared to be stone hard men, who would kill at the drop of a hat, and not feel a second of remorse over it, but that mainly they didn't seem too smart. They had what Johnson called 'book larnin', but not much else,' and could do sums and spell and such, but had no real understanding of or sympathy with other people.

They talked on into the night, until Bass finally called an end to the story-telling and ordered everyone except Stern, who was by now doing his stint of guard duty, to get some rest, for they had a long ride come the morning.

5.

They were up before the sun the next day. Jackson stoked the fire and fixed a meal of hot trail biscuits, beans, fried strips of beef, and coffee. After everyone had eaten, prisoners included, they parted company with Johnson, who again, in his laconic cowboy way, thanked them for their hospitality, and invited them to drop by and see him in Muskogee the next time they were riding through the area.

Eight miles west of their camp site, they came upon a small settlement, not yet a town, but clearly becoming one, consisting of a general store and saloon, the only two fully-finished wood frame buildings, and several tents and partially finished buildings, housing a barber shop, a hardware and notions store, another saloon, and sundry other merchants. The place looked like it had a population of around three hundred people, mostly, it appeared, farmers who worked as sharecroppers on Chickasaw tribal lands around the settlement.

They stopped at a tent which sat in front of a wood rail fence with a crudely lettered sign announcing that it was a combination livery stable-blacksmith shop. The proprietor, a muscular half-breed who looked part black, part Indian, with his kinky hair off his face by a red bandanna, came out of the tent when they arrived. When he saw Bass he smiled, displaying a mouth with more gaps than teeth.

"Hi y'all," he said. "What kin I do fer you today?"

"Howdy, yourself," Bass said. "We's just passin' through, but if would be nice if we could water our horses."

The man pointed at a rough wood water trough at the corner of the fence.

"Help yourself. Water's free. You want me to check your horses' feet? Make sure they ain't got a loose shoe, or a rock stuck between shoe and hoof?"

"Naw, we already done that. I would like to ask you a few questions, though, if you don't mind."

"Shoot, I ain't got no customers right now, so I reckon you kin jest ask away, mister."

"We's lookin' fer a bunch of outlaws, the Dawkins gang. I heard they might've passed through this way. You seen anything?"

"Well now, I sho nuff did. Say, ain't you that fella, Bass Reeves?" Bass nodded. "I done heard a lot about you. First colored man to be a deputy marshal, and all. Ain't never thought I'd lay eyes on you, though."

"Heck," Bass said. "I wasn't the first, I don't reckon. Marshal Fagan, he done hired 200 new deputies, and a whole bunch of 'em was colored. I was just part of the batch."

"Whatever. You still famous in these here parts. Now, this here Dawkins bunch; don't know iffen it was them, but a buncha fellas did come through with a small herd 'bout two days back. They stopped here 'cause one of they horses done throwed a shoe, so they had me put on a new one."

"They say where they was headin'?"

"Naw, they didn't talk much, kinda unfriendly, really. But, with them cattle they was drivin' I'd say they was bound for Fort Sill."

Bass described Clint Dawkins from the description Marshal Fagan had read to him from the wanted poster. The blacksmith smiled.

"You got the boss of that outfit right enough. A mean lookin' cuss, too. Eyes like a snake. I swear I don't think I ever saw him blink."

"I appreciate the information," Bass said. He took two bits from his pocket and tossed it to the man who deftly caught it.

"Ain't no need to pay me, mister, I ain't done nothin to earn this."

Bass smiled. "Naw, you earned it, my friend." He

touched a finger to the brim of his Stetson. "You have yourself a good day now. Come on, boys, we got us some ridin' to do."

6.

Less than two miles west of the settlement, they picked up a trail that both Bass and Henry were sure had to have been made by the Dawkins gang. Cattle, grass eating animals, do two things that irritate most cow herders, and they do them while moving, they pass a lot of foul-smelling gas, and they excrete that part of the grass that their multiple stomachs doesn't digest. The gas dissipates, but the manure picks up dust as it hardens and turns into flat, lumpy rocks that lose a lot of their foulness when they dry and make a fairly decent bit of kindling out on the plains where trees are scarce. The presence of dozens of these cow patties strung out along a half-mile stretch of level ground could only have been left by a herd on the move. The presence of shod-hoof marks mixed in among the cattle tracks was even more convincing.

Bass and Henry squatted near a pile of drying manure.

"From the way it's dried out," Henry said. "I'd say it was left here less than three days ago."

"That means they ain't far ahead," Bass said.

Henry looked up at the sky. The sun was a bit past its high point, but not quite at mid-afternoon.

"I'd say before dark if we push it."

"Maybe we ought to leave Jake, Alvin and Harvey with the prisoners, and you and me ride on ahead."

"You sure just the two of us can take on the whole Dawkins gang?"

Henry had known Bass to take some long chances, and in truth, the man seemed to be blessed by the Great Spirit, having escaped certain death on many occasions, and despite the number of times outlaws had taken shots at him, including one time his saddle's horn had been shot off while he was sitting in it, he'd never been hit. But, against vicious outlaws like the Dawkins gang, could his luck run out? Henry thought about it for a few seconds, and then made up his mind. Stern and Steadman were good men, but the two of them wouldn't change the odds all that much.

"On second thought," he said. "I reckon we probably can. We should find a good place to camp and get them set up."

7.

There was no suitable camping spot nearby, and Bass didn't want them setting up too near any settlement, to prevent danger to civilians, or cause them to have to contend with people coming to gawk at the chained-up criminals, so the prisoner and cook wagons stayed with Bass and Hank for ten miles.

They came to a suitable-looking area, a slight bowl in the earth through which a stream flowed, with a few stands of evergreens and hardwoods, and sufficient grass for the animals. The only problem was that it was already occupied.

They saw a covered wagon, tilted to one side, two oxen, and three people near the stream. White smoke from a fire drifted lazily upwards.

"This looks like a good place," Henry said.

"Yeah," Bass said. "But, I don't like that there's people already here."

"Maybe they'll be leaving come morning."

"Let's go ask." He turned and shouted back at Steadman, who drove the lead prisoner wagon. "Y'all slow down and give us time to find out who them people are down there. Then, we'll wave you on down."

Instead of slowing down, Steadman brought his wagon to a halt, stopping the two behind him.

"Well, you can't get much slower than that," Henry said.

Bass shrugged. "Suppose so. Come on, let's see what we got down there."

What they had was a young man in his late twenties, his very pregnant wife, who looked to be still in her teens, and a toddler, just starting to walk on his own, two oxen looking like they were ready for the meat wagon, and a wagon with a broken left rear wheel.

The toddler looked fascinated, but the adults had

frightened expressions on their faces as Bass and Henry approached. The young man's hand hovered over an old shotgun propped against the left front wheel.

"No need for that, young fella," Bass said. He flipped up the collar of his jacket so that his badge was visible. "I'm Deputy US Marshal Bass Reeves, and this is Henry Lone Tree, my posse man. We're on our way west of here to arrest some wanted men."

The young man visibly relaxed, but still stared at Bass.

I didn't know there was any colored lawmen out this way," he said.

"Yeah, quite a few. Judge Parker over in Fort Smith done hired us, mainly to bring law to the Injun Territory. Where you folks from, and where you headin'?"

"We be the Lanes, George and Clara, and the little twig here is Albert. We hail from Gallatin, Tennessee, and are on our way to homestead in Oregon."

"That's a mighty long way to go for a single wagon," Bass said. "And, mighty dangerous to boot."

"We were gonna turn north at Fort Sill and go up to Kansas City and join a wagon train, but as you can see we had a bit of a problem."

"How'd your wheel get broke?"

"Things were going just fine until this bunch of men with a herd of cattle overtook us yesterday. The oxen got spooked by so many other bovines and started shying. Well, that got that herd to acting up, and they stampeded and one of 'em stumbled into our wheel and broke it."

"Didn't the cowpokes herding the cattle offer to help you fix it?"

George Lane snorted. "Help us? By Jove, no. In fact, the leader of the bunch, a real mean man, blamed us for spooking his cattle. They just rounded them up and rode away, leaving us here to fend for ourselves."

Bass recognized Clint Dawkins' handiwork. The man left a trail of misery everywhere he went. No sense, though, in letting these naïve youngsters know how close they were to death, because Dawkins had been known to shoot a man down for stepping in front of him on the sidewalk outside a saloon.

"Henry, you pretty good with stuff like this," Bass said. "Whyn't you take a look at these folks' wheel and see if we can fix it."

Henry nodded and slid from his horse. The younger Lane walked up to him as he squatted to inspect the broken wheel and ran a pudgy hand over his face. Henry smiled, showing a mouthful of bright white teeth, which caused the youngster to double over giggling.

"Your friend's pretty good with children," Lane said. Little Albert doesn't usually cotton to strangers, but he seems fascinated by him. He's an Indian, right?"

Bass grunted assent. "Yeah, he's from one of the tribes that live here in the Territory since the government took they land back east." He wanted to say, so that white folks could farm it, but there was no sense blaming these youngsters for what some bewhiskered old men in Washington did in the name of progress. "He ain't got no kids himself, 'cause he can't find a squaw who'll put up with him. Me, now, I got me nine, no, ten young'uns back home in Arkansas."

"You must miss them," Clara Lane spoke for the first time.

"Somethin' awful, but this here job of bringin' law to this lawless land, like Judge Parker wants done, means I got to spend time out here away from 'em. It feel powerful good to git home, though."

"I'm looking forward to making a new home for our family," she said, rubbing her stomach.

"I don't think that young'un gon' wait 'til you gets to Oregon from the looks of things."

The young man scratched his head. "I think you're right. We might have to stop in Kansas City until after it's born."

"More like you gon' have to stay a spell in Fort Sill," Bass said. "I don't watched my wife with child ten times, and I can tell you, this wife of yours ain't but a month away at most, and that's less time than it'll take you to get up to Kansas City in a wagon pulled by oxen."

"There are places to stay at Fort Sill? I'm no soldier."

"Aw, just outside the fort is Lawton. Ain't much to look at, but it's a growin' town, and it's got some cheap hotels and rooming houses that'll put you up. Got some good doctors, too."

Lane looked to be thinking over Bass's suggestion. Henry stood, brushed off his pants, and patted the little boy on the head. "It's cracked plumb through," he said. "But, with some rawhide, I can patch it back together good enough to get you to Fort Sill. You get there, though, you will need to buy a new wheel."

George Lane looked like he wanted to cry.

"I don't know how to thank you gentlemen," he said. "I'd just about given up and dreaded we might die out here."

"T'aint no need to thank us," Bass said. "Out here on the frontier folks look out for each other. That cattle drover you run into is the exception, 'cause most people out here know that the only way to survive is to help you neighbor, so when you in need he'll help you."

Watching Henry wrap the splintered wheel back together with some of the rawhide he kept in his saddle bags, Bass wondered if this family would survive the rigors of a wagon train ride from Kansas to Oregon, through some wild country, when they couldn't even cope with being broken down on the road here in Indian Territory. Instead of making a decent camp, they'd just started a fire and sat down near their wagon waiting for someone else to come along and solve their problem. If winter caught them on the Kansas plains, a snowstorm in the mountains of Colorado, or even a dust storm here in the Territory, they would surely perish. If not for the two children, one barely walking, and one not yet born, he would just ignore it, and go on about his business, but when it came to children, Bass had a heart as big as the wide-open plains.

"You know, you folks might want to think about settling down near Fort Sill for a spell," he said. "Least ways until the young'uns is old enough to take a long wagon train ride."

"But, what would I do," Lane said. "I'm, or rather, I was, a clerk for my father's lumber mill back home. I know a bit about farming and raising stock, but not much else. How would we make a living in a place like Fort Sill?"

Bass wanted to scream. If he couldn't make it in a populated area, with soldiers just a stone's throw away, how did he think he was going to make it on a homestead, miles away from his nearest neighbor, and likely no law less than a week's ride away? If this had been one of his sons, he'd be administering a severe tongue lashing, but this was a stranger, and one in distress at that, so he decided to be polite.

"Man what can keep books can always find work 'round a army post," he said. "In town, too, for that matter. I reckon you apply yourself, by the time this new young'un is ready for the trip, you'll done piled yourself up a nice little nest egg."

"Hm, you might be right. What do you think, Clara?"

"Well, I was worrying about such a long trip in my condition, or with a suckling. I think we should take the deputy's advice."

"We'll do it, then. Thank you, deputy, thank you

very much."

Henry had finished reattaching the newly repaired wheel. He now stood aside and let them have a look at it.

"Like I said, it'll take you to Fort Sill, but it will need to be replaced before you try to go any further."

Clara Lane invited them to stay and join them for supper, but Bass informed him that the fugitives he was chasing were getting farther away. He and Henry wished them luck and went back to round up their wagons and crew.

The little boy jumped up and down and pointed as they rode past, and the parents waved, but stared with eyes wide when they saw the prisoners peering at them through the bars of the prisoner wagons.

8.

An hour from where they encountered the Lanes, they arrived at a small settlement of about two hundred people. Bass chuckled at the thought that George Lane was less than a half-day's walk from help if only he'd had the gumption to explore his surroundings. From the droppings they saw on the trail, they figured also that they were less than a day behind Dawkins and his men.

A crowd milled around on the dirt track that passed through the center of the settlement, and even from a distance of a hundred yards, Bass could see that they were not happy. He held his hand up, stopping the wagons.

"Y'all better wait here whilst I go up and see what's goin' on," he said.

"You want me to go with you?" Henry asked.

Bass thought about it. He could be riding straight into a mob, not a smart thing for a man of color to do, even if he was a deputy U.S. marshal. Henry, on the other hand, was a resident of the territory. His presence might forestall any rash actions.

"Yeah, maybe that ain't such a bad idea."

Bass arranged his coat so that his badge was plainly visible, and then riding slightly hunched in the saddle to minimize his otherwise imposing appearance, he and Henry rode toward the crowd.

The hum of conversation stopped as they approached.

A beefy looking young man with a bushy black beard stepped from the crowd.

"Who are you?" Then, he saw Bass's badge. "Oh, you're the law. It's about time you got here."

"What's goin' on?" Bass asked.

"Don't you know? We sent a man over to Chickasha to report it? Ain't that why you're here?"

"I'm here chasin' after a gang of cattle rustlers that were passing this way, so no, I don't know what our problem is."

"We done had a killin', that's the problem. Bunch of rowdy cowhands come through. They were drinkin' and playin' cards with some of the locals in the saloon, when Ned Shaeffer accused the leader of that bunch of dealin' from the bottom. Fella just up and shot 'im in the face. Then, they lit out."

Bass described Clint Dawkins.

"Yeah," the man said. "That's him. That's the evil-eyed snake that shot Ned. What you gon' do about it?"

"Well now, when I catches him, and takes him back to Fort Smith, that charge will be added to everything else he's done, so 'stead of bein' sent to the federal pen in Detroit, he'll likely hang."

"Hangin', hell, that sounds too good for that buzzard. He oughta be throwed in a pig pen and let the hogs eat him."

Bass shuddered at the idea. He'd seen what was left of a body thrown to the hogs, and there wasn't much to see. The omnivorous pigs had eaten everything but the victim's skull, and that was only because they'd come upon the scene before they'd cracked it enough to get the pieces in their maws.

"That ain't a nice thing to think about doin'," Bass said. "Why don't we let Judge Parker and the court take care of punishin' him?"

"That's if you catch him. You sure you can do that?"

Henry spoke up, "This is Bass Reeves, the most feared deputy marshal in the territory. He always gets his man."

The man cocked his head to the side. "Well, in that case, good luck to you."

9.

Bass sent Henry ahead to scout for signs of the gang and resumed his place at the head of his little wagon train. Stern and Steadman had resumed griping about staying in the territory so long, and now some of the prisoners were complaining about being confined to the prisoner wagons like animals for so many days.

"Just hush up, all of you," Bass said. "We be headin' home by tomorrow, day after at the latest. I don't know why you prisoners complain', though. Once we get to Arkansas, they gon' lock you in a cell where you won't be able to see the sun. Least ways, now, you can smell the fresh air and see the sky."

A couple of the harder prisoners snorted at Bass, but the younger ones, those who had yet to experience their first time behind iron bars, looked apprehensive. Bass felt sorry for them, many of whom had been led into a life of crime by older relatives, or circumstances over which they had no control. But, his sympathy only went so far. After a point, he reckoned, a man has to take personal responsibility for his actions, especially when it's been pointed out to him—in their cases in the form of wanted posters—that his actions are wrong.

He shook the thought from his mind. Once they were delivered to the federal jailer they were no longer his concern. Besides, by then, he'd be busy out looking for the next bunch.

As was often the case when he was long in the saddle, his mind wandered, flitting about like a butterfly in a field full of spring daisies, lighting on thoughts of Nellie and his kids, then flitting off to dip into thoughts of his own childhood, sent early to work in the fields because he'd been uncommonly big for his age, and then pulled mostly out of the fields because he was big for his age and good with his hands or with guns, and he was a quick learner, always listening and remembering what he heard.

I just wish sometimes, he thought, that I'd got me a little book learning to go along with the other things.

His reverie was interrupted by the sight of a rider coming at them from the west, a rider that long before anyone else would've seen enough to recognize, he realized was Henry. His horse was galloping, but he didn't seem to be in a particular lather.

When Henry reached them, he turned his horse and rode alongside Bass.

"I found 'em," he said. "They are camped in a glen about ten miles ahead. Looks like they are settlin' in for the night."

"Well now, ain't that nice and accommodatin' of 'em to wait for us to catch up," Bass said. "Lead us to 'em."

"We should get there just at dusk, Bass. You plan on takin' 'em today, or doin' like you did with Greenleaf, and hit 'em at first light?"

"Don't get too dark this time of year 'til seven, so if we get there right at the start of dusk, I reckon we go ahead and round 'em up tonight. That way, we can start back home first thing in the mornin'."

Henry dipped his head in acknowledgment. When Bass decided on a plan, that was it. No further conversation was necessary.

"How we gonna guard the prisoners and help you round up them rustlers at the same time?" Stern asked.

"You ain't. You gon' hang back and watch these prisoners. Henry and me gon' go round these folks up."

"I think it would be easier if there was at least three of us," Henry said.

"Okay, then," Bass said. "We stop short of where they camped, and Alan, you watch the prisoners. Jake, you come with me and Henry."

Steadman grumbled at being left out of the action.

"What you grousin' about?" Stern said. "You still gon' git the same pay I git, and you don' have to git shot at."

That shut Steadman up fast.

"All right," Bass said. "Let's move out."

After forty minutes, Henry called for a stop.

"I think we should leave the wagons here," he said.

Here was a broad pasture with sweet green grass, a line of young oak trees lining the side farthest from the road and dotted with pine trees. The only thing it lacked was a stream, but they'd filled their water barrels and had enough for two or three days.

"Okay Alan, keep everybody quiet until we git back," Bass said. "Jake, git your horse, and come on with me and Henry. We got us a buncha rustlers to catch."

The three of them then rode forward, with Henry leading the way. At a point where the road made a sharp turn north, Henry raised his hand to stop them, then put a finger to his lips for silence. Not that he needed to, because the wind was blowing from the northwest, and the unmistakable odor of cattle was heavy in the air. In addition, they could hear the lowing of grazing cattle.

"I think we should go on foot from here," Henry said.

They dismounted, taking their rifles from the saddle scabbards as they dropped to the ground.

"Okay," Bass said. "Henry, you lead the way."

Henry took them through a small stand of evergreens, the pine needles muffling any sounds their boots made, until they came to the edge of the trees. They looked out onto a broad expanse of natural pasture, a platter-shaped area that sloped gently upwards on the north. A herd of about forty head of various breeds of cattle grazed contentedly under the watchful eyes of four men on horseback who rode around the periphery, nudging the occasional stray back into the herd.

"Seems to be two missing," Henry said. "When I found 'em, there were six."

"Well, let's get these four, and we'll worry 'bout the other two later," Bass said.

They stepped out of the grass, rifles aimed in the general direction of the riders.

"Put your hands up, and don't do nothin' stupid," Bass yelled.

10.

The first of the outlaws to see three men walking from the trees with rifles pointed his way, dropped the reins and almost fell off his horse.

Foolishly, instead of reaching for the reins and steadying himself in the saddle, the man went for the sidearm at his waist. Without breaking stride, and shooting from the hip, Bass put a rifle slug through the man's right shoulder, sending him tumbling over his horse's rump to land on the ground, luckily on his uninjured left shoulder. He scrambled to his feet, grasping his wounded right shoulder and ran for his horse to escape the milling cows, spooked by the shot.

Seeing what happened to their friend, the other three outlaws raised their hands and waited meekly as Bass, Henry, and Stern approached.

The three were quickly handcuffed. They patched up the wounded man, who gave his name as Jack Tatum, and helped him back into his saddle. Under the watchful eye and menacing rifles of Henry and Stern, the four men looked warily at Bass as he walked around and stood in front of them.

"Where is Clint Dawkins and the other member of your gang?" he asked.

The four outlaws looked back and forth at each other, finally, Tatum spoke up.

"Clint and Billy, they done rode on ahead," he said. "He said he was goin' to make contact with the fella what was gonna buy these cows from us."

Bass looked around. In addition to being a mix of breeds, he noticed several different brands.

"So, you fellas didn't steal all these animals from one place, I see."

"We didn't steal nothin'," Tatum said. "These steers was bought all legal like."

"I suppose you have the bills of sale?"

"The wha-, uh, Clint's got the papers."

11.

Bass knew a lie when he heard it, and Tatum wasn't even a particularly good liar, with his blinking and looking away when he spoke.

"Well, they look like stolen cattle to me," Bass said. "So, we gon' take you and them back to Fort Smith and let old Judge Parker sort it out. So, your boss went on ahead to Fort Sill, did he? When did he leave?"

"Just 'bout an hour 'fore y'all come."

Bass and Henry shared a look.

"Jake," Bass said. "You think you can git these four back to the prison wagon by yourself?"

Stern patted his rifle.

"One way or t'other, I can," he said. "Whether they's all alive when we git there kinda depends on them."

The four outlaws all spoke at once, promising they wouldn't try anything.

"Leave the cattle here for now. Me and Henry will drive 'em to you when we come back."

"You goin' after the Dawkins brothers?"

'Yeah. Job ain't done 'till them two's in chains and in one of the wagons."

"Jest two of you ain't gon' have much chance agin Clint and Billy," Tatum said. "Them two is stone killers. Just a day or so ago, Clint shot a man in the face just for callin' him out for cheatin' at cards."

"That charge will be added to cattle rustling," Bass said. "Although, I reckon it ain't nice to call a man a cheat."

"Problem is, Clint was dealin' from the bottom," Tatum said. "Bold as brass and wasn't even tryin' too hard to hide it.

Henry grunted. "We might not be able to bring these two in alive," he said.

Bass shrugged. "I'd rather bring 'em in alive, but if

they don't want to come peaceable like, then we'll leave 'em dead. Either way, they rustlin' and killin' days is just about over."

12.

By pushing their horses, Bass and Henry caught up to the Dawkins brothers in just over two hours. It was dark by the time they arrived and the campfire the two men had built beside a broad, but shallow stream was visible from almost a mile away. They stopped their horses.

"It's gon' be hard to get up on 'em without 'em knowin' we's here," Bass said. "But, I got me an idea that just might work."

"You plan to sneak up on 'em on foot?"

Bass shook his head. "Naw, I'm gon' ride in, but I want you to cut 'round the other side jest in case they try to make a run for it."

"Wait. You plan on riding into the camp of two killers all by yourself."

"Sure 'nuff. If these boys think like I think they do, they ain't gon' see no danger from an old colored cowboy, 'leastwise, not at first. I'll try to get the drop on 'em, and you can come in and back me up."

Usually, Henry didn't question Bass's plans, but he looked at him with a frown on his bronze face.

"I do not think that's a good idea, my friend. What if they just decide to shoot you, whether they think you are a danger or not?"

"Stop frettin', Henry. I ain't been shot yet, have I?"

"There is always the first time."

"Aw, I think this'll work. Now, you git. I'll give you ten minutes 'fore I move in."

Still shaking his head, Henry wheeled his horse to the left and started making his way past the camp site.

Bass gave him fifteen minutes just to be on the safe side. Then, he kneed his horse's shoulders and started forward, making sure to ride 'small in the saddle' the way he'd been taught by the elders of the tribe during his time in the territory during the war. Not only did this seem to shrink his six-foot-one frame, making him look shorter and less imposing, but it also made him a more difficult target for an ambusher.

Clint and Billy were sitting around a fire sharing a bottle of whiskey they'd bought in the last settlement just before they had to leave quickly after Clint shot a local gambler for accusing him of cheating. He *had* been cheating but felt that the man had no right to accuse him in such a loud voice, embarrassing him in front of the whole saloon. The remains of their meal, hardtack and fried pork, was congealing in their tin plates near the fire, and they were deep into the bottle of brown liquor. For that reason, Bass was inside the circle of light from the fire before they heard the clop of his horse's hooves or saw him.

His reactions slowed by the whiskey, Clint, the older brother and leader of the Dawkins gang, clumsily drew his sidearm, a Colt Peacemaker like the two that Bass had under his jacket. Billy, drunker than his older and bigger brother, simply sat there staring wide-eyed at the stranger.

Bass raised his hands, palms facing outward in the universal gesture of surrender. "Hold on, mister, I ain't meanin' you no harm," he said. "I'm jest a weary traveler who smelt that there hard tack and pork settin' on the ground, and I swear I also smelt me some whiskey, less'n I'se mistaken."

Clint aimed his Colt up at Bass, the barrel wavering.

"I don' like nobody sneakin' up on me, boy," he said. "I done shot men for less'n that."

Aw, boss, I wasn't sneakin', or nothin' like that. I reckon you musta been takin' a sip when I rode up. That's why you didn't see me."

"What's your name, boy? Where you from?"

"My name, boss, is Beauregard Reed, and I come up from Paris, Texas," Bass said. He often gave a false name, keeping it close to his real name so he wouldn't forget in the middle of a conversation.

"Where you headed, boy?" Billy Dawkins asked, still sprawled on the ground near the fire.

"Why, I'se on my way up to Fort Sill, young master. I hear they's hirin' guides."

Clint Dawkins laughed. "You, a guide? Who the hell ever heard of a colored guide?"

"Aw, I'se actually a pretty good guide, boss. I rode 'long side my boss when him and the other ranchers down Paris way went out agin the Comanches a few years back. Learned to track real good doin' that. I figger I'se a better tracker than any of them boys they got in the army, that's for sure."

"Well now, don't that beat all."

"I think we oughta jest shoot 'im, Clint," the younger brother said. "What iffen he tells folks 'bout us when he gits to Fort Sill?"

"What's he gon' tell 'em, Billy? That he run into two white men on the road. Hell fire, boy, where's your brain."

"I'm jest as smart as you, Clint Dawkins. In fact, I went to school one whole year longer'n you ever did."

"Ha, that jest means you didn't drop out 'till the fourth grade. Ain't no big deal. Readin' and writin' is way overrated anyway. Wouldn't you agree, boy?"

"Well now, boss, I couldn't rightly say. "Fore 'mancipation, my master didn't allow none of us slaves to learn to read or write. After it was 'lowed, I was too old to go to school."

"You mean you can't read or write, not even a word?"

"Nary a word. So, I can't say whether it's good or bad, 'cause I only know one way."

Clint leaned over to snatch the whiskey bottle from his younger brother.

"I still say we oughta shoot 'im," the younger man said in a whiny voice.

"Oh, shut your trap, Billy. You don't do nothin' but

bellyache. I swear, if you wasn't my brother, I wouldn't have you in the gang. Here, boy, have yourself a drink. As one uneducated man to another, eh?"

As Bass reached for the bottle, his coat fell open. Clint Dawkins got a glimpse of light reflecting off metal. He grabbed the jacket and flung it open, exposing Bass's badge.

"Holy jumping Jehoshaphat, that there is a lawman's badge. What the blazes you doin' with a badge, boy?"

Bass straightened his shoulders and stood at his full height, all pretense put aside.

"My real name is Bass Reeves," he said. "And, I'm a deputy marshal outa Fort Smith, Arkansas. I have me a warrant for your arrest, Clint Dawkins, you and your brother, Billy, both."

"See," the younger man said. "Told you we oughta shoot him."

The elder Dawkins grinned. "Well, for once you got somethin' right, little brother. I reckon I'm gon' do jest that."

He began raising his revolver.

Bass raised his hands again. "Before you shoot me, I'd like to make one request."

Dawkins laughed.

"I reckon the condemned man's entitled to one last request. What is it, boy?"

"When I said I never learnt to read or write, I was tellin' the truth," Bass said. "But, when I come out to the territory, my wife, who can read and write, gives me a letter, even she know I can't read it. 'Fore you kills me, I'd plumb like to know what that letter say, so would you please read it to me?"

"Hell, why not. It's the least I can do."

The younger man stood up and craned to see around his brother's arm as Bass reached into his jacket and withdrew a folded paper. He handed it to the older man, who held it askance to allow the flames from the waning fire to illuminate it. Even though Bass couldn't read, he knew that what he'd handed the man was one of the warrants Marshal Fagan had given him at the start of the trip, probably even the one for him and his gang. Clint Dawkins, for all his bravado, only knew a few words and how to write his name in a barely legible scrawl, and his brother, Billy, was only marginally better, so the two of them stared in puzzlement at the document, not recognizing more than a word or two of the neatly penned warrant.

While they were thus distracted, Bass reached under his jacket and swiftly drew out his two Colt Peacemakers that had fortunately not been exposed when his coat was opened.

By the time the Dawkins boys realized that they were not holding a letter written by a woman to her husband and looked up at Bass with angry scowls on their faces, they found themselves staring down the business end of two revolvers just inches from their noses.

"Now," Bass said. "It look like you ain't gon' get to kill me today. In fact, I'se placin' you two boys under arrest and takin' you back to Fort Smith with me, so jest reach down real slow like and undo your gun belts and let them shootin' irons drop to the ground. And, don't you be thinkin' on doin' anything foolish, 'cause I can't miss from here, and the slugs from these two will take most of your head off."

At that moment, Henry rode into the camp. When he saw the Dawkins standing with their hands in the air and their gun belts at their feet, he laughed.

"Dang it, Bass," he said. "Could you not have waited for me to get here. I never get to have any fun."

13.

After putting on cuffs, Bass and Henry helped Clint and Billy Dawkins onto their horses and took them back to join the other prisoners.

Upon arriving at the camp, Bass saw that Stern and Steadman had also rounded up the stolen cattle. When the four riders entered the camp, Steadman let out a whoop.

"Well, Lordy merch, you done caught 'em," he said. "Now, we can go home."

The injured man, sitting glumly slumped against the wagon wheel to which he was attached by a chain, looked up in surprise.

"Clint, Billy, how'd them two get the drop on you?"

"This boy done tricked us," Dawkins said. "Plumb got the drop on us when we wasn't lookin'."

'You are lucky," Henry said. "You might have had the chance to go for your sidearm, in which case, you would be dead now."

"Oh yeah, says who?"

"You still do not know who has captured you, do you? This is Bass Reeves, the most feared lawman in Indian Territory. He has never failed to capture any outlaw he goes after. A few have tried to resist, even to kill him, and a few of them are dead. The others are in the white man's prison far to the north."

"Bass Reeves, eh. Yeah, you said that was your name. I seem to recollect hearin' that name somewhere."

"If you have been in the territory for any time, you will have heard the name. Spoken in quiet fear by outlaws, and in respect by the law-abiding folks who wish you outlaws would find some other place to go, so that we may be left in peace."

"We come here, 'cause Injun Territory ain't got no white man's law."

"You could not be more wrong," Henry said. "The white man's law is here, and it comes in the form of a black man."

"I ain't never heard of no black lawman before."

"Well, now you have, and you will have a long time in prison to think about it."

"He probably won't spend too long in prison," Bass said.

"After all that he has done, why not?"

"He done kilt a man in cold blood. That there's a hangin' offense, and even though Judge Parker ain't no fan of hangin', iffen the law says you got to hang for what you did, he don' send you to the rope. Now, the rest of 'em, that's another matter, except old Greenleaf, there, who also done kilt and is probably gon' hang, the rest though, gon' be up there in Detroit for a long time."

"What you gon' do with them cattle?" Clint Dawkins asked.

"We takin' 'em with us to Fort Smith. After that, it up to the judge or the marshal what they do with 'em."

Dawkins was bigger than his brother or any of his men, but he still had to look up to meet Bass's gaze. He glared up at him, his chest puffed out.

"You lucky, boy, you know that," he said. "Iffen you had'na pulled that trick with that paper, I'd of put a slug in that black gut of yours, for sure."

"Maybe, maybe not," Bass said. "Luck for both of us, you'll never know. Now, all of y'all get some rest, 'cause we got a long three-day ride ahead of us."

14.

The three-day ride turned into four when a wheel came off one of the prisoner wagons as they were traversing a stream with a rock-littered bed, and they had to spend a day waiting for a blacksmith from a nearby community to fix it.

But, finally, the convoy of three wagons, forty head of cattle and two riders on horseback, rode up the curving road that circled the courthouse to the entrance to the federal jail in the back of the building.

Marshal James Fagan stood just outside the door to the jail wing, frowning and pulling at the ends of his mustache. He was still frowning when Bass dismounted and approached him.

"Mornin', marshal," Bass said. "Fine day, ain't it?"

Fagan continued frowning as he looked past Bass at the milling herd of bovines and the prisoners, their chins down toward their chests as they were hauled off the wagons and lined up to be marched into the jail.

"Quite a crowd you brought back, Bass," he said. "Where'd you get all the beef?"

"Caught the Dawkins gang red-handed, I did. They was drivin' this herd to Fort Sill where they was gon' sell 'em to the army."

"Hm, and two wagons of prisoners. I guess that explains why you're a week past due gettin' back."

"Had to take the extra time to chase Dawkins down, then there's that fella, Greenleaf, who done kilt a mail rider over in Chickasaw Nation."

"Is that a fact?

"Yeah, and he been runnin' liquor into Indian Territory to boot."

Fagan shook his head.

"Bass, you are truly a piece of work. I send you out to roundup fugitives, and you take me literally, and try to rid Indian Territory of every outlaw in one trip, and

185

then you round up a herd of stolen cattle just to confuse the issue. What am I gonna do with you?"

"Well, marshal, if I might be so bold, you could sign off on my trip report so I can go collect my rewards and get on home to Nellie and the chilluns."

Fagan tried holding his frown, but it was impossible in the face of Bass's innocent look as he spoke. That a man his size, with his deadly skills could have such a childlike attitude about life never cease to amaze and amuse him. His cheeks turned red with the effort, and finally he began laughing.

He laughed until his sides hurt. Then, he took a deep breath, wiped his eyes and held out his hand. "Give me the dang papers, and I'll sign 'em. And you get on home, 'fore that woman of yours come looking for my scalp for keeping you gone so long."

Fagan had Bass turn around and he used his broad back as a surface upon which to place the papers so he could affix his signature. That done, he handed them over, shook his top deputy's hand, and watched him walk away.

As the jail guards took charge of the prisoners, he looked again at the milling cows. He turned to the head jailer.

"Get these danged cows penned up somewhere before they cover the yard with their droppings, will you?

The man looked thunderstruck. Accustomed to incarcerating people, he was at a loss when it came to dealing with four-legged creatures. But, Fagan had spoken, and he would somehow find a way to comply.

Darn that Bass Reeves, the jailer thought. Leave it to him to bring back a jailhouse full of prisoners *and* a herd of smelly, loud cows.

BOOKS BY THIS AUTHOR

Lincoln Croft Treasure Hunter

Treasure in the High Sierras
Night of the Blood Moon
Pinkerton's Last Ride
Guns and Gold
Under a Bleeding Sky

Caleb Johnson Mountain Man

Back to Bear Creek
Menace in the Mountain Mist
Snowbound
The Last Wagon Train
Vendetta
Fire on the Mountain
Fast on the Draw
The Tenderfoot

Bass Reeves: The Indomitable Lawman

The Indomitable Lawman, Volume 1

Harry Hooker, P.I.

The Girl's Gone Missing

Al Pennyback mysteries

Color Me Dead
Memorial to the Dead
Deadline
Dead, White, and Blue
A Good Day to Day

The Day the Music Died
Die, Sinner
Deadly Emotions
Death by Design
Till Death Do Us Part
Deadly Dose
Dead Man's Cove
Dead Men Don't Answer
Deadly Paradise
Kiss of Death
Death in White Satin
Death and Taxis
Deadbeat
A Deadly Wind Blows
Death Wish
Deadly Vendetta
A Time to Kill, A Time to Die
Dead Ringer
Death of Innocence
Dead Reckoning
Murder on the Menu
Over My Dead Body
Bad Girls Don't Die
A Deal to Die For
The Dead Blonde in the Red Bikini
Return to Dead Man's Cove

Ed Lazenby mysteries

Butterfly Effect
Coriolis Effect
The Cat in the Hatbox
Negative Side Effects
Murder is as Easy as ABC
Body of Evidence
Who Killed Henry Hawkins?
Skeleton in the Closet

Buffalo Soldier

Trial by Fire
Homecoming
Incident at Cactus Junction
Peacekeepers
Renegade
Escort Duty
Battle at Dead Man's Gulch
Yosemite
Comanchero
Range War
Mob Justice
Chasing Ghosts
The Piano
Family Feud
The Lost Expedition
The Iron Horse
Park Patrol

Jacob Blade: Vigilante

Avenging Angel
Vengeance is Mine
Hot Lead, Cold Steel
The Vigilante From Texas
Hell in the High Country
Last State to Mesa Grande
Shootout at Heartbreak Ridge
A Fine Day for Dying
Vigilante League
Last Man Standing
Bullet from the Vigilante
The Guns of Jacob Blade
Vigilante Killer on the Run
Cold Steel
Heartbreak Ridge Shootout

The Last Stage Heading to Mesa Grande
The Last Gunfighter Standing
Sins of the Father
The Guns of Jacob Blade Vigilante
Vigilante Killer on the Run
The Crow's Shadow
Gun for Hire
Blazing Guns

Other Fiction

Angel on His Shoulder
She's No Angel
Child of the Flame
Pip's Revenge
Wallace in Underland
Further Adventures of Wallace in Underland
Dead Letter and Other Tales
The White Dragons
The Dragon's Lair
Dragon Slayer
The Last Gunfighters
The Culling
Frontier Justice: Bass Reeves, Deputy U.S. Marshal
Angel on His Shoulder – Revised Edition
Battle at the Galactic Junkyard
Mountain Man
Devil's Lake
Vixen
Awakening
Chase the Sun
The Lady's Last Song
Dead Letter and Other Tales – Revised Edition
Catch Me if You Can
A Cowboy's Christmas Carol
Hard Ride to Glenrose, Texas
Toby Giles: Tarnished Badge
Marshals of Dusty Saddle (short story anthology)

Sheriff B.J. Kincaid: Shoot Fast or Die
Guns Along Carson's Ford (with Fred Staff)
Sheriff B.J. Kincaid: Cry of the Raven
Breath of the Dragon
Sheriff B.J. Kincaid: Bullet for a Bad Man
Toby Giles: The Walls of Jericho
Tom Steele: A Day of Reckoning
Sheriff B.J. Kincaid: Showdown at High Noon
The Blazing Guns of the Lawman Kincaid
Toby Giles: One More River to Cross
The Calico Cowboy
Rendezvous at Red Rock Canyon
Tom Steele: Into Dark Lands
Caleb Wolf: The Missing Mail Order Bride
Tom Steele: Demons at Dawn
Caleb Wolf: The Saga of One-eyed Jack
Caleb Wolf: A Date with Death
The Nearest Town is Purgatory
Esau Brown and Jacob Hardin – Leaving Purgatory
Sheriff B.J. Kincaid: Gunsmoke and Glory
Wagons West: Daniels's Journey
Wagons West: Trinity
Sheriff B.J. Kincaid: Gunfight at the Silver Dollar Saloon

Nonfiction

Things I Learned from My Grandmother About Leadership and Life
Taking Charge: Effective Leadership for the Twenty-First Century
Grab the Brass Ring
African Places
A Portrait of Africa
There's Always a Plan B
In the Line of Fire
Advice for the Insecure Writer
Looking at Life Through My Lens
Ethical Dilemmas and the Practice of Diplomacy

Making America Grate Again
DC Street Art
Things I Learned from My Grandmother, Second Edition
Feathers, Fur, and Flowers
Backyards and Byways
American Heroes
Invasion of the Swamp Creatures
Ethical Diplomacy and the Trump Administration

Children's Books

The Yak and the Yeti
Samantha and the Bully
Molly Learns to Share
Where is Teddy?
Catie and Mister Hop-Hop
Tommy Learns to Count
Catie Goes to School

Writing as Ben Carter

William Coburn: Cowboy vs the Sea Monster

ABOUT THE AUTHOR

Charles Ray began writing fiction at an early age, winning a Sunday school magazine short story writing contest when he was thirteen, his first national publication credit, which hooked him on writing. During his stint in the army from 1962 to 1982, he occasionally moonlighted as a newspaper and magazine journalist, and was editorial cartoonist for a small weekly newspaper in North Carolina during the 1970s. In addition, he was an artist/cartoonist, and photography for a number of publications, including *Ebony*, *Eagle and Swan*, and *Essence*, and did covers for *Buffalo*, a now-defunct magazine that was dedicated to showcasing the contributions of African-Americans to U.S. military history. He current writes a weekly column, *Ray's Ruminations*, for a daily and weekly newspaper in Bacolod City, Philippines. A member of the Foreign Policy Research Institute's board of trustees, he's also chair of the institute's Africa Program.

When he retired from the army in 1982, he joined the U.S. Foreign Service, and served as a diplomat in Asia and Africa until his retirement from government service in 2012. He has traveled throughout the world, and visited every continent except Antarctica, and now, as a full-time writer and creative, bohemian sort (he grew a beard to underscore that point), he continues to travel the glove looking for interesting things to write about, draw, or photograph.

A native of Texas, he now calls Montgomery County, Maryland, a suburb just outside the District of

Columbia, home. Check him and his works out at the following sites:

http://charlesray-author.com/
http://charlieray45.wordpress.com/
http://charlesaray.blogspot.com/
http://www.flickr.com/photos/charlesray45/
http://www.viewbug.com/member/charlesray/

Authors write to be read, and that can only happen when readers are made aware of what they've written. Reviews on Amazon, Goodreads, and other book-related sites are one of the best ways to get the buzz started on books. If you've liked this book, take a few minutes to leave a brief review. Thanks in advance.